POISON TREE

Also by Amelia Atwater-Rhodes

DEN OF SHADOWS
In the Forests of the Night
Demon in My View
Shattered Mirror
Midnight Predator
Persistence of Memory
Token of Darkness
All Just Glass

THE KIESHA'RA
Hawksong
Snakecharm
Falcondance
Wolfcry
Wyvernhail

Amelia Atwater-Rhodes

POISON TREE

DELACORTE PRESS

Visit us on the Web! randomhouse.com/teens

Educators and librarians, for a variety of teaching tools, visit us at randomhouse.com/teachers

Library of Congress Cataloging-in-Publication Data
Atwater-Rhodes, Amelia.
Poison tree / Amelia Atwater-Rhodes. —1st ed.
p. cm.
Summary: Alysia has quickly moved to a position of responsibility in SingleEarth, working among shapeshifters and witches who fight against vampires, but she is hiding secret alliances that could put her fellow mediators at risk.
ISBN 978-0-385-73754-8 (hc) — ISBN 978-0-385-90672-2 (glb) — ISBN 978-0-375-98572-0 (ebook) [1. Vampires—Fiction. 2. Shapeshifting—Fiction. 3. Supernatural—Fiction.] I. Title.
PZ7.A8925Poi 2012
[Fic]—dc23
2011030166

The text of this book is set in 12-point Loire.
Book design by Jinna Shin

Printed in the United States of America

10 9 8 7 6 5 4 3 2 1

First Edition

Poison Tree *is dedicated to my wife, Mandi. Her love and support helped me through many revision-related rants and breakdowns, while her feedback and insight helped me untangle several snarls in the story itself. As I write this, we have just celebrated our one-year anniversary. She hasn't given up on me yet.*

As always, I owe profuse thanks to my writing group: Shauna, Bri, Zim, Ria, and last but far from least, Mason. Mason has been one of my strongest supporters—and greatest critics—throughout Poison Tree's *editing process, constantly needling me to reexamine the characters and the story line.*

Like most of my books, Poison Tree *required research into a bizarre variety of topics. Though this list is by no means complete, I would like to thank Karl for his weapons support, Bri for her archery instruction, and Devon for his technological expertise.*

Finally, I must go back to 2002 and thank the cast and crew of Tiger Eyes, *especially Ollie, who instigated that project, and Sam Kruger, who prodded me to develop a story I might otherwise have given up on long ago. You all helped me see and hear these characters in a way I had never expected.*

POISON TREE

I was angry with my friend:
I told my wrath, my wrath did end.
I was angry with my foe:
I told it not, my wrath did grow.

And I watered it in fears,
Night and morning with my tears;
And I sunned it with smiles,
And with soft deceitful wiles.

And it grew both day and night,
Till it bore an apple bright.
And my foe beheld it shine.
And he knew that it was mine,

And into my garden stole
When the night had veiled the pole;
In the morning glad I see
My foe outstretched beneath the tree.

—William Blake, "A Poison Tree"

PROLOGUE

SIX YEARS AGO

THERE WAS BLOOD on her hands, congealing slowly. The body in her arms was cold, its once-vibrant cheer forever vanished from the world.

The dead girl had a thick rope around her throat, attached to a chain hooked into the wall. Sisal bonds held her wrists behind her back. If she had been able to shapeshift, that rope would have burst or blended into her form, but the innocent eleven-year-old girl who had been bound, beaten, and murdered had been human, nothing more.

I failed you. I'm so sorry.

The survivor looked up at the sound of a stifled gasp of pain; someone was moving across the room, through a pile of what she had thought were dead bodies. She couldn't summon fear, not with a corpse in her arms that had once been a little girl she had sworn to protect.

The vampire pushed himself to his hands and knees slowly, painfully. Though bones broke the bloodied surface of his skin, he still moved toward her and said, "We have to get out of here."

She remembered this one now. He had spoken up against his leader and refused to help torture the human girl.

If he had been anything more fragile than a vampire, he wouldn't have survived his leader's response, but now his bones were knitting back together. She knew how that felt; as a pure-blooded shapeshifter, she healed almost as quickly. She could have survived everything they had done to Cori's poor human body. But Cori . . . Cori was just dead.

"What's your name?" the vampire asked as he crawled toward her.

"Sa-Sarik," she stammered, a jolt of fear going through her at last. She was harder to kill than a human, but that didn't mean she wanted anyone to try.

"I'm Jason," he said. "Help me and I can help you. There's another door, but I can't get there on my own like this, and I don't have time to heal before they get back."

She looked around. Once this had been a wine cellar, but now it was just dry and cold, and reeked of blood, fear, and pain. How could she abandon her sister here?

"It's too late to help her," Jason said. "Come on. We need to go."

There was blood on Alysia's hands. Some of it was slick red—which meant it was probably hers—and some was swiftly drying, caking, and turning to dust, which meant it belonged to her prey.

Alysia didn't know exactly who this nest of vampires had pissed off, but she did know that it was someone with enough money to offer a good price. Given what she had been told about this group's behavior, Alysia might have done the job for pennies. Then again, she *did* have a reputation to maintain—and important toys to buy. There was no need to make a charity case out of some rich vengeance-seeker's problem.

Sneaking up on a creature who could hear her human heartbeat and smell her blood would normally have been tricky, but this group had spilled a great deal of blood lately, sating their hunger and dulling their senses. They were also distracted by their own concerns and were whispering among themselves about their most recent assignment, which clearly had shaken up a few of them.

Alysia waited until one had walked away from the others, and then she stepped up behind him and drove a slender steel stake hardly larger than a pencil into his back, beneath his shoulder blade. The tip found his heart unerringly. When she twisted the implement and removed it swiftly, the barbs on the tip shredded the once-vital organ and the vampire dropped without a sound.

Three down. Five to go, she thought. Eventually, they would realize she was there, but each one she took out before they did was one fewer face-to-face fight.

"You!"

Five on one, not the best odds, she thought, spinning toward the voice, only to discover that the vampire who had shouted was not talking to her.

Poacher, she thought indignantly. This was *her* job. What was worse, the jerk who had cut in was obviously an Onyx boy: brash, bold, with no concept of stealth. The black cross-bow he had slung over his shoulder was an Onyx trademark; that guild tended to favor long-distance weapons and rarely jumped into an up-close fight when they could avoid it.

As one of the vampires noticed her and cut into her path, though, she decided she was magnanimous enough to share. Let this Onyx newcomer distract some of them while she picked the others off, one by one.

There was blood on the girl's hands and face, but that didn't seem to distract her as she crept up behind the vampire Christian had been fighting and, with one swift backstab, took the creature down.

"Thanks," Christian said, the only word they exchanged as they instinctively moved back to back. They didn't know each other, but they knew their common enemy.

The girl obviously favored stealth, but she held her own as the three last vampires surrounded them. Christian fought with a long dagger in his right hand; the girl he had stumbled across fought with two weapons: in her left hand, a stiletto, and in her right, a steel stake with rings near the end that served as brass knuckles. He and the girl each dispatched one target, then turned together toward the last.

The vampire put his back to the wall, trying to keep them both in sight, but he didn't flee. He had to know running was his only chance of survival when faced with two Bruja mercenaries, but his fear of his employer apparently outweighed his instinct for self-preservation.

Behind his impromptu partner, Christian noticed a blood-slicked pair making their way quietly across the back of the room. The girl was letting the guy lean on her. She wasn't his prisoner, and more importantly, they were both obviously too injured to fight even if they hadn't been trying to sneak away.

Christian almost called out to them but then decided to let the battered and bruised runaways limp to freedom thinking they had never been spotted. If they spared a backward glance, it was only after he had returned his attention to his fight.

"Nice work," he said as the girl he had been fighting with landed the final, killing blow.

She looked up at him, almost an eye-roll, as if unsure whether he was patronizing her. "You didn't do too badly yourself, for an Onyx brat," she answered, the words paired with a challenging grin.

He glanced past her, but the prisoners had already made their exit.

"Want to get a coffee?" he asked, on impulse.

She lifted a brow, considered giving a snarky answer, and then said, "Offer chocolate and I'll say yes. I always want chocolate after a hunt."

There was blood on Sarik's hands, and it was driving Jason crazy. He had refused to feed from the tiny human girl they had been ordered to kidnap, which meant he hadn't fed in days. Healing the injuries left by Maya's displeasure had weakened him even more. Maybe, if Sarik was grateful . . .

"I need to get this off me," the shapeshifter said, her voice trembling.

They had holed up in a run-down motel that was the first place they reached that didn't seem like it would also be the first place Maya looked. Now Sarik pushed past him and fled to the bathroom. He heard water running as she washed blood—hers, the dead girl's, and his—from her hands, face, and hair. The water stopped, and he thought she might emerge, but instead he heard the door lock, and then the shower running again. With a vampire's sense of hearing, he could easily make out the sound of sobs beneath the hissing of the water.

It's a good thing I don't mind cold water, he thought, looking at the blood on his own hands.

An hour passed before Sarik emerged dripping wet, wrapped in a towel, and announced, "My clothes are covered in blood."

"What do you expect me to do about that?" he demanded.

She flinched, but then fire rose in her eyes, and she snapped, "I saved your *life*. Is it too much to ask for you to hit a gift shop?"

"I thought *I* saved *your* life."

"You couldn't even *walk*."

So he went to the touristy store down the road, wondering why he was even still with her. She was no one, a shapeshifter running away from home who had crossed into the wrong territory and gotten herself in trouble. Maya liked shapeshifter blood, called it sweet and spicy, so she had grabbed this one without hesitation.

The nearest gift shop had closed hours ago, but snapping the lock wasn't hard. He picked clothes up indiscriminately, deciding that a large T-shirt and some sweatpants would be good enough for her to go out and find her own stuff.

She didn't complain when he returned and handed her the bundle, but instead disappeared into the bathroom for a few minutes before emerging in blue sweatpants that read SALEM STATE COLLEGE in large orange letters and a pink T-shirt emblazoned with a huge black lobster. Both were far too large, dwarfing her in their folds.

Jason couldn't help it. He started laughing.

A lip quiver, a half smile, and a few seconds later, so did she.

CHAPTER 1

NOW

SARIK LOOKED UP at Jason with a grateful smile when he placed a cup of hazelnut coffee with a dollop of heavy cream next to her, and was startled by his brief kiss. She had been so absorbed in the papers she had been drowning in for the past hour that she hadn't noticed he had left.

Next, he handed a steaming black coffee to a petite Asian girl who looked fourteen but in reality was the oldest person in the room. Lynzi was a Triste, a type of witch with the same physical agelessness as the vampires. She liked her coffee so strong Sarik couldn't take a whiff of it without her eyes watering.

A fruity herbal tea with honey went to Diana Smoke, the witch who ran their organization. Unlike Tristes, Macht witches were as mortal as any human, but despite the fine lines that had recently begun to appear at the edges of her eyes, Diana had a presence that always made Sarik feel like she could be closer to immortal than any of them.

"Thank you, Jason," Diana said as he set the tea in front of her.

None of them asked if Jason wanted anything for himself. Vampires could drink or eat anything they wanted, but they didn't need to, and Jason rarely chose to indulge just for the taste. The woman who had changed him, and claimed to own him, had set strict rules about such things. Even now, six years after he had escaped her control, he still tended to be nervous about breaking those rules.

He also tended to anticipate and respond to the wishes of those around him, like making a beverage run and returning with everyone's favorite without being asked. The thought that his constant consideration had been taught to him through fear made Sarik's next sip of her coffee bittersweet.

"Israel said you asked for this," he explained to Diana as he handed her another bulky file from the records room.

Diana nodded. She had been alternating between the files on the table in front of her and her phone, which periodically chirped to tell her about an email. "I may have found an applicant worth looking into," she explained. "Central recommended her and sent over her file."

SingleEarth Central, located outside Burlington, Vermont, was the nexus of the international SingleEarth organization, and Sarik's hopes rose at the notion of a recommendation from them. Surely they had found a better candidate than anyone from the endless line of people who had applied for the open mediator's position at Haven #4 as if it were some kind of résumé-builder.

Diana handed out copies of the new file, still warm from the machine.

"Her name is Alysia Marks. She has been in SingleEarth for about two years now and has been in the Technology and Communications department at Central for the last eighteen months. She recently overheard a call she thought sounded suspicious, and when the staff at Central dismissed her concerns, she went to investigate on her own. She ended up spending two hours in a hostage situation with a panicked young man who had just learned about shapeshifters and decided to take drastic measures. According to witnesses, Alysia was the one who talked him down and convinced him to turn himself in to authorities. She also managed to take identifying information from all the victims so our crisis teams could follow up with them."

Everything Diana said about this Alysia Marks made her sound like a perfect candidate for mediator, but Sarik's first glance at the file made it obvious that the witch had left out a *lot*.

"I'm sorry, but have you read the rest of this?" Sarik asked, startling even herself. "It says here that SingleEarth's hunters forced her to resign because they viewed her as 'a loose cannon, unpredictable, taking unnecessary risks.'" She looked up at the others. "Plus, she has a juvenile arrest record about a mile long."

Lynzi replied, "It's common for people—*especially* younger

people—to act out when they learn that humans are not alone on this earth. It also isn't unusual for people to have trouble transitioning when they *do* finally make it to SingleEarth." The remark was directed at Jason and Sarik. They had caused a few waves with their quick tempers and frequent spats when they had first joined SingleEarth four years ago. "The issue with the fighter's guild was two years ago, when Alysia had just joined. I don't see any disciplinary actions or other negative marks on her file since then."

"You're right," Sarik admitted. "Who we are in Single-Earth often has little or nothing to do with who we used to be. But I'm not seeing any evidence here that she even *wants* this job. Did she apply?"

She had not. There was, however, a note indicating that she had applied for a promotion in the Information Technology department, which included everything from network support to document acquisition. Jason and Sarik both had birth certificates and Social Security cards provided by that group—SingleEarth's own form of witness protection.

"Alysia has been working in IT for almost two years now," Diana replied, "but she has previously expressed an interest in moving into a more people-centered career."

Jason stepped up in his own cautious way. "I share some of Sarik's reservations," he said, "but I see no reason not to invite her in for an interview. We all became mediators because we are better with people than with paper."

"My thoughts exactly," Diana said.

Lynzi nodded her agreement, and with that, the discussion was over. Diana Smoke had made up her mind, and no twenty-two-year-old tiger hired a little over a half year ago was going to override her.

Funny, that was exactly the reason Joseph had cited for quitting, leaving this position available: despite SingleEarth's stated mission of equality, he had felt that witches' voices carried more power. Sarik wasn't sure who he thought *should* have final say, given the fact that Smoke witches had founded SingleEarth, and Diana Smoke was officially the organization's CEO. Witch or not, someone always needed to be in charge.

Sarik realized guiltily that she had been expecting the stereotypical tech geek, but Alysia showed up at SingleEarth Haven #4 wearing a gray suit jacket with black pants and a dark rose button-down shirt. Her brown hair was tied back and clipped up and she looked like a young professional trying to make a positive first impression. Sarik found herself sympathizing with her, despite her earlier reservations.

She's nearly my age, Sarik thought as they shook hands and introduced themselves. *Only a year older. Is she as nervous as I was when Diana interviewed me?*

Alysia did not look nervous as she shook hands with the others around the table. She smiled at the right moments, but the smile disappeared when Diana asked her to describe what had happened at the Café au Late coffeehouse recently. She chose her words carefully, relating the story modestly but honestly.

Why does she seem so familiar?

The thought pricked at Sarik as Alysia was answering

questions about her past, a subject most members of Single-Earth tried to avoid.

"I spent most of my life getting into trouble," she freely admitted. "I'm good at figuring out how things work, and when I was fourteen or so, I didn't care that sometimes it was illegal to make something work—like a car or someone else's computer." The rueful acknowledgment made Diana, Lynzi, and Jason nod sympathetically. "I enrolled in university to study psychology when I realized that people are even more interesting than machines. I discovered that I am good in a role where I can talk to people and help them understand what is going on."

"And manipulate them," Sarik interjected.

Diana shot Sarik a warning look, but Alysia just gave a half shrug. "Sometimes," she answered, meeting Sarik's gaze squarely. "I mean, yes," she continued, her voice rising slightly as she continued. "When I walk in looking for a coffee and there's a guy with a gun, a round of explosives, and a filet knife who plans to keep slicing people up until he gets his way, then yes, I pray to whatever powers might exist that I can manipulate him so we can all walk out of there alive. And I did, and then I got every person who had been in that room into SingleEarth's care within hours so they could decide if they wanted to become shifters and could get the post-trauma therapy one tends to need after spending six hours as a hostage. That's why I'm *here*, isn't it?"

"Indeed," Diana said. "You and Sarik are both right. Sometimes in this organization, it is our job to educate openly, and sometimes it is our job to manipulate in any way possible to ensure the safety of our people."

Alysia nodded.

"You should know," Lynzi said, "that Haven Number Four isn't the type of place that normally deals with things like hostage situations. While we do act as point people in times of crisis, your day-to-day job here is more likely to be spent doing paperwork or getting on the phone to coordinate with hospitals, therapists, and law enforcement within and beyond SingleEarth."

Haven #4 was one of the smallest of SingleEarth's properties, and mostly housed individuals who just needed a safe place to stay. The Haven had a therapist on staff but did not even have fighters; unlike some of the other Havens, they didn't work with the types of individuals who drew violence or caused it. Sarik had chosen #4 for that very reason. She wanted to stay far, *far* away from the other side of SingleEarth, which dealt with supposedly reformed mercenaries and killers and with violently unstable survivors of magical mishaps or of uneducated upbringings that made them unable to control their own bodies and minds.

Alysia smiled modestly. But to Sarik, her expression seemed fake.

"I function well in a crisis," Alysia replied, "but I don't need or want to spend every waking hour living one."

Does she remind me of myself? Sarik wondered as Diana thanked Alysia for her time. The human made her round of polite goodbyes and left.

Everything Alysia had said had been right. Sarik couldn't fault her if it seemed *too* right; she was applying for a job that would require knowing how to say the right thing in the right way. Sarik had walked into her own interview with significantly less experience and far more questionable moments in her own background.

"I like her," she said to the others after Alysia was gone and the door was closed.

It wasn't true, really, but it *should* have been, because Sarik had no valid excuse to feel otherwise. Nothing except a vague sense of familiarity and the ever-present anxiety that someday the demons of her past would catch up to her.

CHAPTER 2

BARELY FORTY-EIGHT HOURS later, Alysia stood in the parking lot, leaning against the bumper of her one-year-old Subaru and wondering what on earth had possessed her to accept this job.

For the last two years, she had worked in SingleEarth's IT department. It didn't matter that there wasn't much challenge in it, because it was just a job, an excuse to keep up to date and fill the time before she moved on. This new job, working as a mediator at Haven #4, wasn't glorious, either, but it was an entry-level position on SingleEarth's crisis team, where someone like Alysia could really make a long-term career.

Long-term. Career. There are two concepts I never thought I'd be interested in.

Yet here she was, standing in the middle of nowhere while the brisk December wind cut through her, despite her jacket and gloves. Most of the trees in the forest around her were pine, but there were enough bare branches and old, fallen leaves to give it a tired feel.

Haven #4 was set in the woods of western Massachusetts like some kind of bizarre college campus. The buildings were connected with old-fashioned cobbled paths that always made Alysia wonder why an organization dedicated to peace and inclusiveness for all creatures who lived alongside humanity—shapeshifters, witches, vampires, and other oddities Alysia had only ever heard of—couldn't design a Haven that was wheelchair-friendly.

Of course, Alysia had never met a witch, shapeshifter, or vampire with mobility issues. The witches had even been able to mostly fix Alysia's bum knee, which had gone to hell again after she'd spent hours kneeling on the floor of the Café au Late. She flexed it now experimentally and hoped she would not need to climb too many stairs to move in. The witches could bring down the recent swelling, but magic could not undo scars that her body now accepted as part of itself.

Her introspective pause gave the welcome wagon time to arrive, in the form of two Haven #4 mediators. They re-introduced themselves warmly, as if they were not all standing under an ominous winter sky.

Alysia had looked up the files of her soon-to-be coworkers, so she knew that the young-looking girl who called herself Lynzi had been in SingleEarth since the 1960s and had been walking the planet Earth for almost a thousand years before that. The woman with her was Sarik kuloka Mari, a tiger shapeshifter. The word *"kuloka"* translated to "of the tribe," but Mari wasn't a real Mistari tribe; it was the name adopted by the few tigers who had abandoned the Mistari homeland and culture and chosen instead to live as citizens of the United States.

Sarik's features were the striking blend of African and Asian common among tiger shapeshifters, but she had straightened and lightened her hair so it was a shade paler than Alysia's, and the makeup and clothing she wore dulled her honey-colored, almond-shaped tiger eyes and hid a body built to turn heads. Even her perfume was something subtle and floral, appropriate for a woman whose job was to make people trust her.

Alysia didn't discriminate much by species. At that moment, the important part was that the two nonhuman girls were probably each able to bench-press Alysia's weight one-handed. That was nice, since Alysia had not been looking forward to lugging her belongings inside with only human strength and a bad knee.

"This is all you have?" Sarik asked as she and Lynzi maneuvered a large trunk out of the back of the car. The trunk was too bulky for any one person to carry easily, even if it didn't weigh a ton, but Sarik and Lynzi together were able to manage it. Alysia took her laptop bag and a large duffel containing mostly computer peripherals, which left only one large suitcase behind.

"I'm not much of a material girl," Alysia replied. Someone from Haven #1 had taught her the term. Some people connected it to spirituality and some people connected it to Madonna, but one way or another, they tended to smile or chuckle when Alysia used it.

Alysia's apartment was on the second floor. Lynzi unlocked the door and handed Alysia the key as she explained, "It's nothing fancy, but Haven Number Four is residential, so we have a fitness room and recreation areas, and you have access to all that."

"Almost all," Sarik amended. "There's a section of the grounds currently being used by a pair of orphaned Mistari cubs we took in a few days ago. I'm sure you heard about them."

Alysia raked her memory, but nothing relevant surfaced. "I tried to go over everything I could about Haven Number Four before accepting the position, but I must have missed it."

"An organization-wide memo went out when the cubs were found, calling for someone who speaks their language," Sarik explained. "I assumed you'd have seen it."

"I probably did, but I didn't know any tigers yet," Alysia answered, "so I wouldn't have given it much thought." Single-Earth had thirty-seven Havens in the continental United States, plus one in Alaska and many in other countries. Memos along the lines of "I need an expert in . . ." or "Does anyone speak . . ." shot along the network constantly. "Are there any other important guests I should know about?"

"You met Diana Smoke when you interviewed," Lynzi answered, "but she was only here until we filled your position and will probably head out once she's sure you're settled. Her responsibilities don't let her stay anywhere long. Where do you want this trunk?"

"Just put it anywhere for now," Alysia answered as she set her bags on the couch. The one-bedroom apartment wasn't a palace, but it was a huge step up from the studio she had previously rented. It was also fully furnished and rent-free because mediators were expected to live onsite.

At the sudden intrusion of classical music, each of them glanced toward their phones—except Alysia, who had surrendered her company-provided phone at Central and was still waiting for #4 to provide the smartphone upgrade they had promised.

Lynzi's first words after "Hello" were "Yes, I'm with Alysia." Alysia's ears were not good enough to pick up the reply, but obviously the conversation was not intended to remain a mystery for long. "Keep her there. I'll bring Alysia right down. Thanks." Lynzi hung up and, shaking her head, said, "That was Mary, from the admin building. I'll show you the way. Sarik, do you mind bringing the rest of Alysia's stuff up?"

"No problem," Sarik answered. She asked Alysia, "Do you want me to lock up after, or just leave the keys inside?" Alysia didn't need to speak; her reaction must have shown on her face. "I'll lock up," Sarik said. "If I can't find you, I'll leave the keys at the front office."

"I imagine it's a bit of culture shock, coming here from Central," Lynzi remarked as they left the apartment.

"A bit," Alysia admitted.

"After we see what Mary needs, I'll give you a tour of the

place and introduce you to some of our residents," Lynzi assured her.

Can she possibly be as nice as she seems? Alysia wondered. There were not many Tristes in SingleEarth. Her experience with them so far had shown most of them to be powerful beyond comprehension, and arrogant enough to match. Yet Lynzi seemed to be happy playing tour guide.

The lobby of the administration building was utterly nondescript; it could have been any office waiting room. Chairs and couches offered comfortable places to sit and wait while reading one of the popular magazines on the coffee table. The back wall had pamphlets for advocacy and support groups. Some were well-known domestic violence hotlines and shelters, like American Humane. Others described symptoms of "rare" diseases that tended to actually mean the patient had blood that wasn't entirely human. The pamphlets didn't say anything about magic or the paranormal but suggested appropriate people to contact about relevant symptoms.

The woman there waiting for them, flipping through a pamphlet on psychorizia, was dressed in a snappy skirt suit and jacket and was—as far as Alysia knew—completely human.

"Madeline Brooks, isn't it?" Alysia asked, offering an open smile and a handshake to the anchorwoman of one of the national news stations. CNN, ABC, something or other; Alysia couldn't recall which one. "I'm Alysia Marks. What can I do for you?"

Alysia was almost certain she knew exactly what had brought Madeline to SingleEarth, because she had recently put quite a bit of effort into avoiding this woman's camera crew—not entirely successfully, though at least she had only been a nameless background figure instead of an interviewee.

"I'm trying to do a follow-up to Tuesday's coffee shop holdup," Madeline said. "One of the victims gave me your information."

Like many successful reporters, Madeline had a warm, glowing smile and the kind of aura that invited those around her to open up and speak freely. The feeling she inspired was a lie and a trap, but Alysia had always been good at guarding her tongue.

"I would love to help you out," Alysia said, "but I'm afraid that any information I have is privileged. Why don't I give you the contact information for our public relations department? They can tell you more about our organization."

"Your own story wouldn't be privileged," Madeline said. "How did you happen to be there?"

"I was just trying to buy a coffee," Alysia said, with the same innocent charm that had helped her talk her way out of interrogation rooms in the past. "I gave my card to the others because my organization works with trauma survivors, and being held hostage is a traumatic situation. Mary," she said, turning to the receptionist, "would you help Ms. Brooks here schedule an interview with PR? I'm sure she would love to hear more about our support groups." With a smile, she turned back to Madeline and added, "It's always great to get the word out." She offered her hand, which Madeline shook, because that was what common courtesy demanded. "Now if you'll excuse me, I'm late for another appointment. Madeline, thank you so much for your time."

Alysia might have been at this particular Haven for less than an hour, but even a lowly member of tech support knew SingleEarth's company line for reporters. The good people at public relations would feed Madeline Brooks an appropriate story about trauma survivors and the hardships faced by homeless shelters. They would also point her toward organizations that would make a better story for human prime-time news and appreciate the spotlight.

Lynzi followed Alysia into the office in the next room, as if she were the person there for the appointment Alysia had just invented.

"Don't you think you should stay to make sure she's effectively sidetracked?" Lynzi asked.

Alysia shook her head. "As long as I'm in her sight, she'll want to make me the story."

Lynzi nodded.

As a Triste, Lynzi could have just wiped Madeline's mind of any interest in Alysia, but she had pointedly stepped back and let the newcomer handle it. That wasn't trust; it was a test.

"So, did I pass?"

Lynzi feigned surprise for half a second before laughing and saying, "Yes, you passed."

"How often do people around you forget that you're the senior member here, and probably the most powerful?" Alysia asked. It was the most polite way she could think of to ask about *what* Lynzi was. Tristes were so rare; it had been surprising to find one in this out-of-the-way spot.

"Most people do—once," Lynzi answered. "It's why my teacher chose me. Do you know much about Tristes?"

"A little," Alysia answered. "I had a friend a while back who was offered training."

Tristes were like vampires, in that they were not born but made. The process of training and initiating a student was much more intensive than with vampires, however, who were often made and discarded at a whim, only to be picked off by hunters not long after.

"Offered by whom?" Lynzi asked.

"Pandora," Alysia answered, knowing exactly why the mention of that name made Lynzi wince. Pandora's methods had left scores of survivors—if some of the worst could even be called that—in SingleEarth wards with broken minds and bodies.

"I was taught by Tatiana," Lynzi said, "but I am familiar with Pandora's ways. If you ever want to talk, I'm here."

Alysia nodded, startled by the compassion and openness in Lynzi's response. She *shouldn't* have been startled—this was SingleEarth, after all—but though she had spent two years at Central, that complex was a small city in itself, with lots of room to get lost in and many people minding their own business.

Lynzi must have sensed the awkwardness Alysia felt, because she turned away and set her hand on the windowpane as she remarked, "We should make sure all your belongings are inside and get your keys back from Sarik, before the storm breaks."

CHAPTER 3

THE SLEET SLAPPING against the windows had woken Jason well before sunrise, two hours after he had fallen asleep at midnight. He slipped out of bed and away from Sarik, who muttered an incoherent protest, grabbed his pillow, and continued to sleep.

Sarik had been anxious the entire day before, so he was grateful that she slept now. She had asked for a meeting with Diana, only to be denied when an emergency came up at another Haven. The only thing she had confided to him was that Alysia looked familiar.

Alysia had admitted that she had been no angel before she came to SingleEarth, and everyone knew her file was full of unaccounted-for time. Alysia was a stranger to Jason, though, and unlike Sarik, he had a vampire's regrettably perfect photographic memory to call upon as he looked at the newest member of SingleEarth Haven #4.

Still, Sarik's anxiety had rubbed off on him, and now he felt restless.

He crossed soundlessly into the living room and left the bedroom door open a crack so Sarik would know he was still nearby if she woke. It had been a long time since the night terrors had broken her sleep, but the way she tossed and turned before succumbing tonight warned him that they were a possibility now.

Normally, work helped him focus and calm himself, but tonight he was frustrated by an impossibly slow network that continually dropped signal and interrupted even the simplest Web page or download.

Footsteps in the hallway drew him out. He discovered Alysia, bundled up and apparently about to brave the winter weather in the predawn darkness.

"Is the network always this bad in a storm?" she asked the moment his door opened, before she added, "I mean, hello. Is it good evening or morning?"

"Might as well be good morning, and no, the weather doesn't normally affect it."

"I figured I would head over to the admin building and see if I could figure out what's going on."

"I already called," Jason said. "Mary has a tech support guy on the way."

"I *am* tech support," Alysia protested, "or I was two days ago. I might as well try."

"I get that, but you're human, and it's nasty out there," Jason replied.

Alysia didn't flinch at the reference to her species, like many SingleEarth members did. Jason filed that information away in the mental list he kept of what soothed or upset the people around him. He had already figured out that Alysia spoke diplomatically when she thought the situation demanded it but preferred bluntness from those around her.

"Let me leave a note for Sarik, and then I'll check in the admin office to see what's going on."

Alysia nodded reluctantly. The spark in her eyes said she wanted to work out her frustration by fixing the problem herself, but she was trying to be reasonable.

The Haven guarded its land in a way that made it impossible to appear or disappear inside any of the secure buildings, but Jason only had to cross the threshold to the porch before he could will himself to the atrium of the administration building.

He found Mary still in the office. She had been there all night, trying to deal with the network issues, but now she was happily flirting with some twentyish guy, who was almost on her lap as he tapped at her keyboard.

"Problem, Jason?" Mary asked, lifting a slightly exasperated gaze that said, *Do you mind?*

"I just wanted to check on the status of tech support," he answered, trying to find a way to back out gracefully.

"Tech support accounted for, though this might take me a while," the guy at the computer answered.

"This is Ben," Mary added.

"Let me show you—" Ben said, starting to speak to Mary before looking up at Jason dismissively. "We're good here. Go get a coffee or something."

Jason nodded and retreated to the records room, which was run by a shapeshifter named Israel. She looked up at him as he entered, blinking in a way that suggested she had fallen asleep at her desk. The admin building ran twenty-four hours a day to accommodate the number of members whose schedules tended toward the nocturnal, but sometimes the routine took its toll, especially when it was cold and dark outside.

From the next room, Jason continued to hear Mary's flirty giggle, until she stopped and called, "Jason, could you come in here?" He heard her add to Ben, "That's more of a mediator issue."

"You've got a virus," Ben said when Jason returned to the front office. "A nasty one. I thought at first that sweet Mary had downloaded too many bootleg naughty movies." Mary flushed bright red at the allegation. "But now I'd say this is intentional. Not surprising, since your whole security system sucks. I can fix it, but first, do you have a place I can crash for a couple? I've been up thirty-six."

Are you speaking English? Jason wondered. Maybe it was the fatigue talking. "We have some extra space in the residential building," he said.

"Residential as in people live there, right?" Ben asked cautiously. "Not residential as in check in and lock down."

"We don't have any locked wards at Number Four," Jason confirmed.

"Great, then!" Ben smiled warmly, though he turned the

expression instantly on Mary. "I'll look you up tomorrow, babe."

Israel poked her head out of the back room. "If you two are heading over to residential, do you mind if I walk with you? I was supposed to be out of here hours ago, and I would rather have company in this weather."

"Don't you need a jacket?" Ben asked Jason as he pulled on an oversized black leather jacket weighed down by whatever gadgets were in its pockets.

Jason shook his head. Despite the absence of pulse or respiration, a vampire's body burned at just above a human's normal body temperature regardless of the environment.

His eyes, unfortunately, could make out little through the icy sleet falling from the sky, so it was a good thing that he knew these paths blind. Israel gripped his arm, and Ben seemed to be using him to block the wind.

The pain came from nowhere, like a bolt of lightning, followed by the searing agony of lava flowing through his veins, into his heart and brain. As he fell, the sleet became needles of ice striking his skin.

He could hear the others shouting as he struggled to open his eyes. Through a red haze he saw that Israel and Ben were both on the ground, Israel dreadfully still and Ben on his knees with a hand pressed over a wound on his leg as he cussed in what sounded like six different languages.

Ben's teeth were chattering as he coughed and said, "We need a—" He broke off, looked up, and shouted, "Alysia!" His whole body shuddered. His voice seemed to get farther and farther away as he continued to shout. "Alysia, you—" He broke off and leaned forward to retch into the snow.

Jason's body was going numb, and his vision was starting to dim. He was only vaguely aware of Alysia hoisting his arm, shouting for Mary as she dragged them inside. The movement seemed to make things in his body stir, and the pain became brilliant once more.

In the light of the admin building atrium, he managed to open his eyes long enough to see that there was something slender and black protruding from his stomach. He wanted to cry out "No, don't!" as he saw Alysia reach for it, but she didn't hesitate before she ripped the weapon from his flesh.

Darkness.

He woke in a dark cellar, body aching, veins burning. Maya had told him that she would leave him this way for as long as it took. As long as what took?

No light, no way to judge the passage of time, only the pain, which turned to madness, to fury and mindless, soul-shattering agony. Even when she came and let him drink from her veins, the pain lessened only a little.

He couldn't remember his own name. Couldn't remember—

"He needs blood," someone said. "I pulled the firestone from his system, but I can't replace the power he lost."

He hissed at the mention of firestone. Nasty poison. Made by Tristes. One of the few materials that could really harm a vampire.

"Alysia, didn't you hear me?" the voice asked. "He needs blood."

"Yeah." Her voice sounded hoarse, reluctant, but she leaned down and pulled him close to her throat, and that was all that mattered. His fangs sliced into her flesh, and then he felt a sweet bliss as the pain finally faded.

Alysia. And that must be Lynzi. I'm still at SingleEarth.

He pulled away with a jolt. Alysia recoiled, though he had taken barely more than she would have lost for a standard blood test.

"You need more," Lynzi said, looking up from tending to Ben, who was mumble-singing something about . . . a llama? . . . under his breath while she worked on a gaping wound in his leg.

Jason shook his head. "I'm fine," he said.

Alysia couldn't know what she had just risked. Had no idea of the nightmare Jason had been reliving in the darkness of pain left by the firestone in his blood. No idea that that slow torture Maya had put him through had ended with a half-dozen corpses on the floor when she had finally tossed human prey into the cellar with him.

CHAPTER 4

SARIK STARED AT the note left next to her bed: *Going to check the network. Be right back.* Since finding it, she had showered and dressed and was now just waiting anxiously, listening to the sound of her own pulse and the sleet battering the window.

He's a mediator. He could have been delayed for a million reasons. There is no good reason to go looking for him.

But I know something is wrong.

She was sure of that, even before the sound of her cell phone ringing made her heart leap into her throat.

"Yes?"

"Sarik, this is Lynzi. I'm calling the Table together, immediately." Her voice was brisk but not strained. Damn Triste self-control. It was impossible for Sarik to know how bad it was by Lynzi's tone.

On the other hand, in the eight months Sarik had been part of the mediator's table, Lynzi had never called an emergency session. That gave her an excuse to ask, "Is everyone okay?"

Lynzi hesitated long enough that Sarik's heart threatened to do the same. "Everyone will be. I'll explain everything once the meeting begins—in my room. Don't go outside."

"I'm on my way."

She shoved her feet into the first pair of shoes she could find, then grabbed a pair of hair-sticks from the dresser top and pinned her hair up as she hurried down the hall.

Lynzi had said "everyone *will be*" all right, not "everyone *is*." People were hurt, very hurt.

Lynzi's apartment was one of the largest in the building. The living room was full of porcelain vases, crystals, and fine sculptures. Sarik did not know what any of them did, but she suspected they were more than just decorative; after all, they belonged to a thousand-year-old witch who maintained these rooms as her ritual space.

Normally, just being in this room made Sarik feel better. Today, the air felt hot and dry; she fought the impulse to rub her arms, as if to brush away a swarm of gnats.

The sectional had been pulled apart to make distinct seats around the coffee table, but only Lynzi and Jason were sitting.

Lynzi was curled up on one of the corner seats with her knees pulled to her chest, so she looked even younger than normal. Her dark hair had come loose from the scarf she wore, and it fell around her sweet-looking face, casting shadows over her eyes. Jason was pale, with dark circles under his eyes. When Sarik ran to his side, he flinched away before saying, "Sorry," and reaching up to grasp her hand. The chill in his skin told her that he still desperately needed to feed.

"You need blood," she said.

He shook his head sharply. "Later."

"What happened?"

Lynzi said, "We were attacked. Just outside the admin building. Jason, Israel, and a technician named Ben were all hit with some kind of arrow—"

"Bolt," Alysia interjected. The human stood to the side of the window, wearing worn jeans, boots, and a long-sleeved turtleneck with a vivid blotch of blood at the cuff.

"Bolt, arrow, whatever," Sarik responded. "*Who* attacked you?"

"We don't know that yet," Alysia answered. "Judging by the angle, whoever it was must have been on the balcony of the recreation hall. Lynzi says some witches might have been able to determine identity through auras or something, but I doubt even someone with a vampire's sight could have made out more than general shapes given the weather, and Jason doesn't see how anyone could have predicted exactly who would be in that spot at that moment. So the targets were probably random."

"What's the difference between a bolt and an arrow?" Lynzi asked. "You said it as if it's important, Alysia."

"It *is* important," Alysia answered. "Arrows are shot by something like a longbow or a shortbow. Modern variations exist, but you might as well think Robin Hood. These were shot from a crossbow."

As she spoke, Alysia stepped forward and unrolled a bundle of fabric that had been on Lynzi's coffee table, revealing three deceptively simple-looking black bolts. The shaft was a little fatter than a pencil, and the feathery pieces on the back were mostly black with gold detail. Each bolt's tip was different: one was solid metal, one had a nasty-looking barbed tip, and one had the distinctive red sheen of firestone. Alysia picked up one of the bolts. Sarik noted that the human did not cringe, even though these had surely been inside someone's flesh not long ago. She twirled it until the light glinted on a phrase written down the side in gold: *One of the former.*

"Who here is familiar with Onyx?" Alysia asked.

Lynzi said, "I've heard of them. They tried to recruit me, around the turn of the century—the last one, I mean. They're assassins."

"Assassins and mercenaries," Jason added. He paused, trying to decide how much Lynzi needed to know. "I wasn't exactly a saint before I came here. I wasn't personally associated with Onyx, but the woman I . . . who I worked for made sure we knew the important names in the game."

"And Onyx is a pretty important name," Alysia said. "They're one of an elite trio of mercenary groups called the Bruja guilds. The phrase on these bolts is a reference to Bruja's motto, and the crossbow is Onyx's signature weapon."

"You seem pretty familiar with them," Sarik remarked. Her own voice startled her. How did it sound so calm? Habit, she supposed. For now, she needed to say the right things, ask the right questions. She could think it through and fall apart later. "Can you theorize why they would attack us?"

"If they're mercenaries, then the only reason to attack is because they're paid to," Lynzi answered. "So the question is, who would *hire* them to attack us? And why?"

"Given the visibility and the wind, the fact that all three shots connected with their targets suggests an expert," Alysia said. "And all three victims are still alive—that suggests that the attacker was very careful *not* to kill."

"That seems like a stretch," Jason objected, his hand instinctively going to a spot low on his stomach. "You saw the bolt that hit me—you were the one who took it *out* of me. It had firestone in it."

"And we had a Triste in the next building," Alysia replied. "Anyone from Onyx planning an attack would have done research first. They would know what we can take. Jason was hit in the lower abdomen, Ben was hit in the leg, and Israel's worst injury was to her hand, which was at her side next to her leg. I refuse to believe this archer could hit all three targets yet somehow aimed too low to connect with any vital organs."

"The stomach is pretty vital, as is the femoral artery," Jason replied.

"Not like the heart, or lung, or aorta," Alysia argued, "and not with the kinds of healers we have on staff."

"You were there?" Sarik asked as Alysia's words sank in.

Alysia nodded, and then seemed to pause. She looked at Sarik, and Sarik could see in the human's eyes the exact moment when she realized that her presence on the scene looked suspicious.

"I went to see if I could do anything about the network issue," Alysia answered.

Before dawn, in sleet and freezing wind, after tech support had already been called? Sarik bit her tongue to hold back the question.

Lynzi frowned and then rubbed her temple. Especially in her own ritual space, Sarik knew, the Triste could probably feel every spike of emotion around her, no matter how carefully someone tried to conceal feelings. On the other hand, with so many strong emotions piled on top of the exhaustion she must have been coping with after healing Jason, Israel, and Ben, Sarik would have been surprised if Lynzi could read anything specific.

Jason squeezed Sarik's hand. He said, "Alysia ran forward when Ben shouted for her. She helped get us under cover, pulled the firestone out of me, and kept Ben from bleeding to death before Mary could get Lynzi. And she donated blood."

Sarik nodded, taking in the information. Jason was right; Alysia's reaction wasn't what she expected of a mercenary.

Lynzi swallowed and said, "I think we need to send someone to Onyx. I'm sure they see us as a bunch of tree-hugging peaceniks, but SingleEarth is one of the wealthiest and most influential organizations in the world. We need to make it clear that there is a value to not crossing us."

Sarik shuddered at the notion and then turned and stared when Alysia said, "I can go and try to set up a meeting. Immediately, unless someone has a good reason to wait." She glanced up at the clock on Lynzi's wall. "The Hall is about four hours away. I can get there and back by evening."

What are you thinking, Alysia? Sarik wished she could read the human's mind. Alysia's knowledge of Onyx made it obvious that she had some kind of history with them. It was possible that she was in SingleEarth because she had run away from that guild, but if so, why would she volunteer to go *back* there?

The panic of the morning was getting the best of Sarik. She didn't have enough information to make sense of Alysia's behavior, but she knew one thing for sure: she needed answers.

"You shouldn't go alone," Sarik said. "You gave blood this morning. You shouldn't be driving four hours to meet with mercenaries."

Alysia glanced at Jason and Lynzi, who were both obviously exhausted. They would need to feed and rest to recover their strength. That left only Sarik.

This is the only way to know, Sarik told herself. She had to risk it.

At last, Alysia said, "I would be happy to have you with me."

"Fine," Lynzi said. "I'm going to update Diana and then call Central to get security here. Onyx may have elite mercenaries, but SingleEarth is *not* defenseless.

"Both of you. Travel safe."

"I wish I could go with you," Jason said softly, standing to come by Sarik's side. He wobbled, unsteady on his feet, and she caught his arm and kissed him before her normal reserved attitude could catch up to her.

"I love you," she said.

"Make sure you come home," he said.

She nodded. "I promise."

CHAPTER 5

THE ONYX HALL had once been a theater, though it had long ago been gutted and stripped down to a skeleton. The scaffolding that had once supported lights and rigging almost eighty feet above the proscenium stage was now only ever occupied by one person.

Christian Denmark leaned against the back wall, comforted by the inky darkness that was never pierced by the dim lights that barely illuminated the main level.

He had been awake for three days straight, training with Pandora. His entire body ached, his head pounded, and his skin was still occasionally streaked with flashes of heat, cold, or simply searing pain. Entering into the deep trance required to resettle his energies was proving nearly impossible, but at least at this hour the Onyx Hall was *quiet*. Most Onyx jobs happened under cover of darkness, so members rarely faced the morning light.

He had thought that such trials would end after his initiation several months earlier, but Pandora never stopped *pushing*. Was near immortality worth the price?

Most people disregarded their other senses as long as their eyes were working, but the leader of Onyx, named Kral, believed it was crucial for members to operate using at least five senses—six, if they could manage it. The Hall was kept in darkness so thick that even a shapeshifter or witch could make little use of what light might become available. Therefore, Christian noticed immediately when the door opened, admitting a band of light.

A member would have stepped inside and closed the door, but in this case, the light remained long enough that Christian chose to investigate. He scrambled down the scaffolding, memories as old as he was letting him know where each bar or beam was without any assistance from his eyes. He dropped the last twenty feet, absorbing the impact without damage, and crossed toward the still-open door.

There were two visitors. One hung back in the doorway; Christian kept his eyes averted from the morning sunlight streaming in around her and turned his attention to the other one, who had walked toward the assignment board.

Any member was welcome to view that board, but the way the other woman lingered in the doorway made it seem more likely that these two were not supposed to be here. He crept closer, sliding up the crossbow hanging at his back so he could balance it on his arm.

A shape shot past him in the darkness, barking frantically. The red Labrador retriever wasn't much of a guard, since he would sooner lick than bite, but Christian smiled nonetheless as the woman at the board stiffened and turned toward the dog.

And laughed.

He froze in the darkness, unbelieving, as he watched her try to calm the exuberant dog, saying things like "Hi to you, too. Get down. No—" She gave up, and her tone sharpened as she gave the command, "Ringo, sit!"

Ringo sat, though his tail never stopped playing percussion on the floor: *Thump, thump, thump!* Christian's heart felt like it was doing the same thing.

He didn't stop to wonder, or think, or watch his back, or question, or even to take an instant to practice any of the self-control that was so crucial for his survival as both a member of Onyx and as a Triste. Instead, he wrapped an arm around Alysia's waist to pull her forward, partly in a friendly greeting along the lines of a hug and partly because he needed to touch her to convince himself that she was real. The words that came out of his mouth—"Alysia, long time no see"—were ridiculously understated compared to his racing thoughts.

The controlled words and tone were a product of more years than he could count of being careful about what other people saw and heard from him. Hearing his own voice startled him back to reality. Alysia was here, but she wasn't alone—and what was she doing here?

"And this is . . . ?" he asked as Alysia pushed him away with a seemingly sad smile. The figure in the doorway still hadn't stepped forward enough that he could see her. Did she know that, at this hour, the light pouring in around her made her featureless to anyone who wished to preserve any night vision?

"Christian," Alysia said, her voice perfectly even, "this is Sarik, an associate of mine from SingleEarth."

SingleEarth! He had a million questions he wanted to ask.

"It's nice to meet you," the other woman said.

Despite the polite words, she did not step forward or offer to shake his hand. Clearly, she wasn't a threat; she wasn't even brave enough to enter the building. She didn't matter.

"Why are you here?" he asked Alysia.

It wasn't the question he wanted to ask. What he wanted to know was why she *hadn't* been there for the past two years. The last time Christian had heard anything about Alysia, there had been a two-million-dollar price on her head. The only thing that kept him from demanding answers immediately was that he didn't know what game Alysia was playing—yet.

"We're here on SingleEarth business," Alysia answered.

He tensed almost imperceptibly as she reached into a pack she was carrying, but the only weapons she retrieved were useless without a crossbow: three Onyx bolts.

"Do you recognize these?"

He did, instantly. He could even tell how old the firestone was, and who had made it, which gave him all sorts of theories that only confused him more. "They're ours," he replied. "Pandora made the firestone."

"How can you tell?" the other woman—what did she say her name was?—asked.

Stupid question. Firestone could only be made by Tristes, and any Triste could read the signature left on it.

"Why bring these to me?" he asked.

Alysia hesitated, which was when Christian realized how stupid he had been.

Alysia hadn't come here looking for *him*. If anything, she would have picked this hour because she knew when the Hall was normally empty. She hadn't wanted to see anyone—or be seen herself.

Was this the first time? Or had she been here dozens of times, even hundreds? Like him, she was a third-ranked member; she had access to private contracts that could be accepted and fulfilled in complete secrecy.

Alysia looked to her cohort, and the other woman cleared her throat as if nervous.

"As Alysia said, we're here from SingleEarth," she said. Her voice was smooth like a politician's, with a meaninglessly friendly tone and a bland Midwestern accent. "Three of our people were attacked this morning with these weapons. Alysia recognized them and said that someone from here was probably responsible."

Christian's patience was running out fast, making him recall all the aches he still carried in his body. "Alysia is probably right," he answered. "What's your point?"

Her carefully controlled tone broke, long enough for her to snap, "Our people could have been *killed*, and—"

Genuinely surprised, he interrupted, "Whoever did this *missed*?"

"They didn't *miss*," she bit out, before taking a step back, swallowing tightly, and getting her voice under control. "Alysia understands the logistics more than I do, but she thinks the archer didn't intend to kill."

There were plenty of people in SingleEarth who might have had enemies from their previous lives—Alysia was a prime example—but Christian couldn't imagine a contract going up to harass SingleEarth's members without a kill intended. Alysia's information was probably good, if she was telling the truth, but since Christian couldn't imagine her in SingleEarth, he had no idea whether she had any reason to lie.

"The shots were professional, easily third-rank," Alysia said, "but I've never heard of a third-rank member of Bruja who would take a job where there's no risk, no glory, not even a body left behind—nothing but panicked, unarmed Single-Earth members."

There was anger in her voice as well, though Christian suspected she was upset for different reasons than her cohort.

"Whoever attacked us used these bolts to send a message they didn't have the courage to present directly. The coward isn't going to get away with it. Understand?"

Alysia kept the words vague, but Christian took the meaning: she didn't know what it was yet, but she was sure that this message had been intended for her.

Us. She had used the word "us." Whoever attacked *us*—her and SingleEarth.

If the message is meant for her, then let her deal with it, Christian thought.

"If someone has a contract out against SingleEarth, I haven't heard about it," he said, "so you might as well be on your way."

"Christian—"

"You might want to leave quickly," he suggested. He pocketed the packet of bolts, noting the way Alysia's gaze followed the movement. "Before someone here decides your intentions might not be in our best interest."

If Alysia really wanted to talk to him, she was going to have to do it at a time and place of *his* choosing, and it wasn't going to include an audience.

For now, Alysia looked from him to the sunlit doorway and then at him again. She started to speak, but then she shook her head and left with her SingleEarth friend. Given the glare of the morning sunlight, it was impossible for him to know whether she looked back.

CHAPTER 6

THERE WERE PLENTY of ways to find anonymous, willing blood donors in SingleEarth, and that was what Jason preferred. He didn't have "regulars," he never accepted blood from friends, and he *never* bled Sarik no matter how many times she offered. He knew his refusals bothered her, but there was no way he could make her understand.

After he fed, there was work to do. Lynzi was still resting, so it was up to Jason to greet the hunters who were arriving from less peaceful Havens. Thankfully, the weather had subsided to a fine drizzle as he showed their new security force around the campus.

"Is this the only video surveillance?" one of the hunters

asked, examining the camera in the lobby of the administration building.

"Yes. It's there mostly to give the secretary a heads-up," Jason explained, aware that the angle was ill designed for security.

The door opened to admit another hunter, who shook drops of water from her hair before she announced, "I cannot imagine anyone making the shots you've described." Though she seemed to be speaking to Jason, she walked past him without looking at him and then spoke to the first hunter. "There are trees close to the recreation building. The weather would have made it hard to climb them, but not impossible."

One problem with SingleEarth hunters was that they tended to start out as vampire hunters, so no matter how long they spent in SingleEarth, they rarely regarded one of Jason's kind as a serious ally.

So no one objected when he left to work on his own investigation.

Of the three victims, only one had a good, predictable reason to have been outside at the time of the attack. Jason was normally sleeping at that hour, and given the weather and the vampiric ability to travel place to place instantly, no one would have expected him to be outside. Israel would usually have left hours earlier, and while it was possible that someone had waited on the icy roof of the recreation building for that long—a vampire or Triste could have managed it—it seemed like an unnecessary, uncomfortable risk for someone to take.

That left Ben, the tech support guy who had showed up in response to a service request generated by a cyber attack. Ben *had* asked Jason where he could get some sleep, but he couldn't have known that Jason would show up in the first place, so it was more likely that Ben was a target than a conspirator.

Jason wasn't entirely dismissing the possibility that Ben was involved, though, for one good reason: Jason had crossed Onyx in the past. If they had found him, he couldn't predict what they would do. Depending on what Alysia and Sarik learned at Onyx, he would decide what the others needed to know about all that.

A look in Ben's file revealed nothing obviously strange. He had been in SingleEarth for years, working mostly with computers and usually frequenting the more urban-style Havens and wards. There was nothing to indicate he had enemies, but such things didn't always make it into the record.

Two birds, one stone, Jason thought as he knocked on the door of the room where Ben was staying.

Lynzi answered.

"I thought you healed him," he said, concerned.

"I didn't have time or energy to fully heal him earlier," she answered. "I was able to stop the bleeding, but then I had to move on to others. There is still work to be done now to avoid long-term damage."

Lynzi stepped into the hall and gently shut the door behind her. "He's sleeping now, though it was a hard battle for me to get him there. He is understandably anxious and wants to get back to Central as soon as he can. He feels safer there. He keeps muttering that this place reminds him of somewhere called Crystal Lake. Have you had any word from Sarik and Alysia?"

"Sarik called when they were leaving Onyx to let me know they were safe. That was almost five hours ago, so they should be back any minute."

Lynzi nodded. "Diana called to check in, too. She's swamped following up with that coffee shop event, but she gave me the authority to sign for any resources we need and assured me that if we need her here personally, she'll be on the next plane."

"Do you think anyone from Alysia's coffee shop could be involved in this?" Jason asked.

"Diana thinks not," Lynzi answered, sounding slightly hesitant. "She says the survivors are mostly coping well, thanks to Alysia's swift intervention, but she has been fielding calls left and right from the media."

Jason's phone rang; he moved farther down the hall, away from Ben's door, to answer.

"Hi, we're back," Sarik said. "Do you know where Lynzi is? Her phone went straight to voice mail."

"She's been with Ben," Jason answered.

"Sarik?" Lynzi guessed. When Jason nodded, Lynzi suggested, "Tell them to meet us in the conference room."

Jason relayed the message, and soon after, they all gathered in their regular meeting room. The cherry-paneled walls and other rustic accents seemed a good deal less peaceful now that Jason had taken a bolt to the guts on the steps of this very building.

"Alysia was looking pretty ragged by the time we got back, so I suggested she lie down," Sarik said.

Lynzi nodded. "Did you learn anything?"

Sarik nodded and chewed on her lower lip, a habit she had when she was nervous. "We met someone at the Hall. His name is Christian. I gather he and Alysia have a history of some sort. He seemed happy to see her at first, but then he more or less told us to go to hell."

"Christian Denmark?" Jason asked.

Sarik shrugged. "Alysia only used his first name. It seemed like the kind of group where asking last names might be a bad idea."

Lynzi nodded, and asked Jason, "You know him?"

"I've heard of him," Jason said. "Christian is kind of like a foster son to the leader of the Onyx guild. It would probably be for the best if he didn't see any more of Sarik."

"Excuse me?" Sarik asked. "Not that I want to make friends with a mercenary, but why me specifically?"

"The leader of Onyx is a tiger," Jason explained. "An old-school heavy hitter with ties to the Mistari high queen, if rumors are to be believed."

Sarik went pale as a sheet.

According to Mistari law, each tribe was a distinct unit under the absolute control of their current king or queen, who answered only to the high ruler back in the main camps. Thousands of years ago, the tribes had specialized in order to provide for the greater community; some were mostly hunters, some gatherers, some planters, some craftsmen, and so on. In the modern age, that translated into some tribes being splendid examples of democracy and art and spirituality, and some being brutal, ruled by a claw-and-fist autocracy.

Sarik never spoke about her past, except in bits and

pieces—usually when she woke from the nightmares left behind by being regularly beaten within an inch of her life whenever she transgressed.

"That could create problems while I'm trying to find a home for the cubs," she said, her voice sounding hollow. "I'm still waiting on responses from the tribes I have contacted."

SingleEarth sometimes interacted with other Mistari, but very rarely with royalty, because Mistari royalty generally disapproved of individuals like Sarik who had chosen to leave their home tribes. If a Mistari king saw Sarik and deduced that she was a runaway, he was likely to report her to her father. Jason wasn't going to let that happen. Ever.

Lynzi nodded her agreement, though she did add, "Sarik, you know that SingleEarth would never let anyone take you without your consent, right?"

Sarik nodded, but the look in her eyes was blank. After years of fear, and pain, and shame, it was hard to fully believe anyone's promise of protection, especially when new violence seemed determined to intrude on the peaceful life they had struggled to build over the last six years.

CHAPTER 7

ALYSIA WAS IN motion before she knew what had wakened her. She made the first several attacks blind, while still blinking the sands of sleep from her eyes. Her mind registered things like movement, the flash of eyes—and a weapon. By the time she recognized the intruder, she had him pinned to the ground with an arm across his windpipe.

She slapped Christian upside the head as she pushed herself to her feet. He was lucky she hadn't been able to get a hand to the knife she had glimpsed at his waist.

No, not lucky. He knew her style well enough that he would have been careful to keep her from any weapons until they both knew she wasn't trying to kill him.

"Jerk," she said with a smile. "That door was locked for a reason."

She offered him a hand up, unsurprised by his sudden appearance in her bedroom. She had given him enough information to track her down if he chose, and had suspected he would follow through as soon as he got over being simultaneously surprised and pissed that she had surprised him.

As he rose, he said, "Was it really?" He took a moment to straighten out the leather jacket he wore and to check the security of items beneath. He might have left his crossbow at home, but Christian was never unarmed, not even in the heart of SingleEarth.

Alysia looked at the clock and then turned back to him with a halfhearted glare. "Five in the morning? *Really?*" She sat back down on the bed, finger-combing hair out of her face. There wasn't even a hint of light outside her windows.

"I didn't want to stay up much later," he replied, "and I wanted a chance to catch you alone."

He reached into his jacket to retrieve a slender package; unrolling it, he revealed the three bolts Alysia had given him at Onyx. "Am I right that these are yours?"

She nodded tiredly. That had been the final joy the day before—discovering that someone had broken into her room. She hadn't unpacked anything but her laptop before the attack, so she didn't know exactly when the bolts had been stolen, but the lax security at Haven #4 would have left plenty of predictable opportunities while she was being shown around the campus.

She fished a key out from between the mattresses and tossed it to Christian.

Christian knelt down to open the innocent-looking trunk, where two framed photos lay nestled among sweaters—one of Alysia's mother in Paris, and one of her father with his girlfriend in Key West. The photos sitting side by side seemed to give the illusion that the individuals within would ever choose to be in the same room together.

Without needing to be told, Christian pushed the sweaters aside to reveal a false bottom, under which were Alysia's real treasures: an Onyx crossbow, with its arms collapsed for storage; three slender metal stakes, each with its own adaptations to make it better suited for fighting; and a set of daggers. Each weapon represented a hard-earned rank in one of the Bruja guilds.

"You've kept them in remarkably good condition for someone living at SingleEarth, but you're likely to lose them if you keep putting them into other members," Christian remarked.

"I didn't—" Alysia drew a deep breath, biting back her defensive retort as someone knocked on the door.

What now? She was halfway across the room before she thought to glance back to confirm that Christian was swiftly concealing the weapons again. "I'm coming," she called out.

She opened the door prepared for the worst and found Lynzi there, wearing pajamas and an assortment of jewelry that seemed at odds with her appearing otherwise recently awakened.

Her gaze went instantly to Christian as she asked, "Is everything okay here?"

"Yeah," Alysia answered, struggling to both wrap her brain around why Lynzi was there and come up with a good excuse for Christian's presence.

"Morning. I'm Lynzi," she said, offering her hand.

Christian glanced at Alysia as he shook Lynzi's hand and said, "Nice to meet you. Alysia, are all your friends such early birds?"

It was a struggle for Alysia to keep her face straight as she realized that she could at least cross Christian definitively off the list of possible shooters. As she had told the others, any Onyx member planning that hit would have done research first.

Christian had obviously forgotten to do his research.

"I sleep lightly," Lynzi explained with a gentle smile. Her tone was still utterly modest and sweet as she added, "I also sleep across the hall, and your veiling is terrible."

Christian pulled back his hand abruptly, his eyes focusing on Lynzi for the first time as he realized she was more than the kid she seemed.

"Your veiling is very good, I gather," he replied.

Veiling was a technique used by witches to make their aura look like something else—usually human. Mortal witches could veil to an extent, but Tristes were the best at it.

"You're Alysia's friend who was training with Pandora?" Lynzi asked.

Seeing Christian's normally impeccable cool broken was fun—and useful, since it was solid evidence that he wasn't responsible for the recent carnage—but it still left Alysia watching the conversation fatalistically.

SingleEarth was all about forgiveness and new beginnings. Lynzi didn't need to believe Alysia had *always* been innocent— just that Alysia's life in Bruja was *over*. And she would believe it, unless Christian said something to contradict Alysia.

I know you're angry with me, Christian, she thought desperately, trying not to fidget, *but please don't screw this up.*

As if he had heard her thought, Christian glanced at Alysia again, this time to check what to say. When she nodded slightly to confirm that she had in fact told Lynzi about a Triste friend, he said, "She knew Pandora had offered to train me. I hadn't made the decision before the last time we spoke."

"So it's been a while," Lynzi surmised. "I gather you're the friend she ran into at Onyx?"

"I was shocked as hell to hear her say she was with Single-Earth," Christian admitted, "but Alysia has always been full of surprises. I gave it some thought and decided I might as well look into this attack she mentioned."

Lynzi nodded. "I'm going to get dressed," she said, "and then I would be happy to show you around the attack area, to see if you have any theories."

"Alysia could do—" Christian broke off in the face of Lynzi's even, determined gaze. "Sure," he said instead.

"I'm right across the hall," Lynzi said before stepping back out of the room.

Alysia snickered as the door closed behind Lynzi, and started rummaging through her bags for clean clothes. "How much would Pandora kick your ass for that mistake?" she asked.

Christian had been human when she'd seen him last,

but even then, he would have kicked himself to next Sunday for making such a stupid assumption. Just because someone looked young and harmless didn't mean she was either of those things.

Christian turned away as Alysia changed from sweats and a T-shirt to dress pants and a chrome-blue button-down. They had lived in close enough quarters that she didn't have a lot of modesty around him, but the fact that he looked elsewhere said a lot. There weren't many people Christian would turn his back for.

"Are you here on a job?" he asked.

"Not a Bruja job," she answered. "I know it's hard to believe, especially since the circumstances make me look guilty as sin, but I'm here as exactly what they think I am."

"A SingleEarth mediator?" Christian asked, incredulous, turning back toward her. "You expect me to believe that? Alysia, you eat adrenaline for breakfast and commit felonies for an afternoon snack. At least, that was the you I knew two years ago—before you disappeared. In the middle of the night. While I was sleeping. I thought you were *dead*, Alysia."

She winced. How could she even begin to explain the last two years? She could explain why she'd left, she supposed. He deserved that much.

"I got a call and went to a meeting for a private contract. It turned out to be most of the guild leadership—Adam, Crystalle, and Kral. They offered me seven figures if I could knock you off and make it look like an accident or a job gone south."

"What did you say?"

"What do you *think* I said?" she snapped. "I told them to

go to hell. In exchange, they doubled the money and put a public posting up in all three guilds—on *me*. I wouldn't have lasted the week. I didn't intend to disappear so long, but then I got involved here."

"And it didn't occur to you to warn me that Bruja leadership was trying to have me killed?" Christian asked.

"You . . ." Alysia trailed off, unsure how to phrase her response. The leaders hadn't put out a contract on Christian because they'd wanted him gone, they'd just wanted to see what she would do. They had made it clear that they believed she was the one rocking the boat and Christian was just along for the ride.

"No, go on," he said. "You refused a million dollars to kill me but then didn't want to waste a minute *calling*?"

"The contract wasn't about *you*," she bit out, "and you know it. Even when you and Kral want to kill each other, you're obviously Bruja raised. I'm the one who came in and started trying to change the status quo. When I refused a million dollars to kill you, the leadership realized it meant that my loyalty couldn't be bought. I knew that if I disappeared, they wouldn't have any reason to go after you. I didn't think they would come after me, either, as long as I was out of their way. But maybe I was wrong," she added, thinking about the recent attack.

"It doesn't matter," Christian said. "Sarta was pissed about the cabal against you, so she competed for and won guild leadership from Crystalle shortly after you disappeared. Then Adam lost the last Challenge—you should have seen the fight that went down there, before Ravyn picked up the Crimson leadership—and I won Frost. Kral's still around, but his teeth aren't as big without Adam and Crystalle worshiping him. You would have allies now. You can come back."

Alysia hesitated, remembering the rush of adrenaline after the attack. Christian was right that she wasn't made for a sedentary life, but despite the two-million-dollar bounty on her head, she wouldn't have stayed at SingleEarth this long if it hadn't offered her something she hadn't found at Bruja.

She had joined Bruja when she was fifteen; it had appealed to her as an angry kid who liked to buck authority and challenge the world and didn't care if she ever got a high school diploma. When she had started wanting to *make* something of her life, she had naturally used Bruja as an outlet. Christian had supported her, but he hadn't really *understood*, just as he wouldn't understand if she told him that she was now three semesters into a double major in psychology and political science at the University of Massachusetts.

Lynzi rapped politely on the door once more, and Christian said under his breath, "There's the babysitter. How old is she?"

"About a thousand," Alysia answered.

"To answer your question, Pandora is going to kick my ass into the next decade," Christian said as he opened the door. "You always did make me leap before I looked."

As Lynzi rejoined them, Alysia found herself simultaneously frustrated and relieved. The instant she had seen Christian at the Onyx Hall, two years had seemed to melt away. It could have been yesterday that they had been fighting side by side.

But she *needed* to remember that those two years had passed.

She wasn't the same person she had been when she'd left Bruja, but Christian hadn't yet realized that. She missed Bruja like crazy, especially on the dull days when she wanted to scream just to get her blood flowing, but she wanted more than the mercenary guilds could provide.

I should be careful what I wish for, she thought as she followed Christian and Lynzi. She had wanted both Bruja *and* SingleEarth, but the only way those two groups would ever come together was with bloodshed.

CHAPTER 8

THE TWO MISTARI children, Jeht and Quean, were obviously brothers, with skin almost the exact same shade of dark russet, and straight black hair. As Sarik entered the enclosure that had been set aside for their use, Jeht prodded his younger brother to wake up, and greeted her: *"Divai, ohne."*

It was a respectful greeting, appropriate for a nearly adult Mistari speaking to a queen in her own territory. The words would have been accompanied by both boys rising to their knees if Sarik had not previously forbidden them from performing such acts of submission.

A Mistari tribe could be run in many different ways, but it had taken Sarik only seconds upon meeting these boys to determine that they came from a tribe where the king's word

was the only one necessary to declare pardon or execution—
and where the only way to challenge that word was a duel
to the death. The hand-forged golden bands Jeht wore on his
upper arms marked him as one of royal blood, even if his posture and direct-beyond-his-years gaze had not. He and his
brother had been driven out of their tribe after the coup that
overthrew their father.

"*Ciacin,*" Sarik replied. In the boys' native language, she
continued, "How are you today?"

"We are comfortable," Jeht replied, focusing on Sarik,
his Asian eyes a distinct golden green rarely seen outside the
Mistari.

Mark, the groundskeeper who had bonded with the boys
and who supervised them—and their campfire—during the
day, stepped forward as if to join the conversation. One ges-
ture from Jeht, however, sent him scurrying away.

Sarik raised a brow and remarked, "He isn't your subject."

Jeht paused to consider the words, and then replied, "He
does not seem to know that. He tends the fire. He makes
us . . ." He paused, saying in English, "Cider." He waited until
Sarik nodded to confirm that he had said the unfamiliar word
correctly. "He brings us our meals."

"He is trying to take care of you." *He sees you as children,*
she almost added. By the standards of the Mistari, Jeht was
almost an adult. He and his brother were also princes. Calling
him a child was not a good idea. She was going to have to talk
to Mark about how to respond to the boy, who had to understand that this world didn't revolve around concepts of master
and subject, strong and weak.

Instead, she said, "You and your brother have been here long enough that you should learn where you can get your own food." Showing them the cafeteria would give them more independence and give them less of a sense that other people should wait on them. Jeht glanced back at the four-year-old Quean, who was watching them sleepily, and Sarik added, "I can show you first, and then you can explain to your brother later."

"As you wish," Jeht answered. He trusted her word that the younger boy would be safe here.

Unfortunately, this particular SingleEarth Haven was currently less safe than Sarik would have liked, even though Mark and the hunters were keeping a close eye on the tiger children.

"While you live here," she explained as she led the way, "you are allowed to have meals in the . . ." She didn't know the word "cafeteria." "A common kitchen and meal room. You can choose what you want."

She did not realize she had said something wrong until she felt Jeht hesitate beside her, and he said in a formal tone, *"Sana'kaen."* Literally, the phrase meant "You make right," but it implied that he was deferring to her authority despite disagreement or distress.

Sarik thought back over her own words and realized what she had said. In the Mistari camps, he had probably eaten with his family and other high-ranking individuals. It wasn't a tradition Sarik's father had bothered with, so she didn't think about it while attempting to translate the concept of a cafeteria. In Jeht's mind, she had demoted him.

"We do not eat by rank here," she tried to explain. "Where

and what and with whom you eat implies nothing about you or your status."

"Quean is very young," Jeht said. "He will learn quickly. I do not want him to learn badly while we are here."

That was the other conversation that needed to be had.

"Jeht . . ." Sarik drew a deep breath before saying, "I think it would be a good idea for you to learn the ways of this place. I am trying everything I can, but so far I have not been able to find a way to get you back to the Mistari camps."

Jeht froze, all expression draining from his face. She reached for him, wanting to be comforting, but he recoiled as he asked, "Then what will happen to us?"

"You are safe here," Sarik said quickly. "As I promised you before, you may remain here as long as you like. Single-Earth will provide teachers, so you can learn local customs, and the language. It is a good life."

"It is a good life for you, but it is not my life," he replied.

In many ways, their native language was much more explicit than English. The fact that he dropped the formal pronoun for her but used one for himself made his full meaning clear.

"I will keep trying," Sarik said, "but in the meantime, I need you to make an effort to—"

"I wish to leave," Jeht said flatly. "If you cannot help us, then we have a better chance of returning home if we do not accept charity from outsiders."

"You can't just leave," she protested. "You're—" *Children.* "You don't know how to survive here."

"Are we prisoners?" he inquired.

She said it this time. "You're children, in this society's eyes. Even if you leave here, you will not be allowed to wander on your own. Someone will call the police again, like they did before, when you were first brought here."

She could see the fury in his eyes, but she could do nothing about it, except hope that he would be wise enough to believe her. Leaving SingleEarth would gain him nothing.

It was a horrible thought, but she realized she was going to need to warn the hunters that Jeht could be just as dangerous as any outside threat. Even a Mistari child could be deadly in a fight, if he thought SingleEarth was keeping him and his brother captive.

What would Sarik have done when she was Jeht's age if she had been thrown out and offered a chance in SingleEarth?

Cori had been four. She had been lively and cheerful, a little quiet, but she had adored her older sister. She had also been just old enough for their father to emotionally disown her when it became obvious that she lacked the ability to shapeshift and for Sarik's mother to storm out in a fury when she discovered that her mate had been fooling around with a human. His having another woman on the side had been forgivable in her eyes, but she had been disgusted that her mate had sullied the pure Mistari blood by mixing it with what she saw as a lesser creature's.

And Sarik . . . where had Sarik been? She hadn't had any idea what life was like for Cori. She lived in a rough world; even at nine years old, she had understood that. Her father had been proud that she had been able to hold her own.

Eventually, his pride hadn't mattered enough. Eventually,

the fights had become too much. Sarik had tried so hard to seem strong, but she'd started to hate the bloodshed more and more. The weakness showed, until her enemies became bold enough to go after Cori.

When Cori had died, it had killed who Sarik had been. But at Jeht's age? Sarik hadn't known any way to live besides the one she'd grown up with. She probably would have killed someone, if doing so had been the only way to get her home.

As if it had been cued by her thoughts, she heard Alysia's voice. Looking up, she saw the human with Lynzi and—

Christian.

She turned toward Jeht, trying to conceal the way her heart was pounding and her mouth had just gone dry. What was he doing here?

He was across the room. He hadn't seen her. He hadn't seen Jeht. She couldn't afford for him to see either of them, so she hastily led Jeht back outside, toward his own territory.

The leader of Onyx is a tiger. An old-school heavy hitter with ties back to the Mistari high queen, if rumors are to be believed.

She remembered Jason's warnings. She had also considered something he had not: if Jeht had known what Jason had said earlier, he would have run to Christian. By protecting herself, Sarik was denying him that chance.

"Give me a little more time," she said to Jeht. "If you want to return to the Mistari camps, you know that you need a king to accept you as part of his tribe. I haven't entirely exhausted my contacts."

The words were bitter in her mouth. Could she do this?

By Mistari law, she had left her father long enough ago that she could declare herself a free woman. He had no claim to her unless she allowed it. On the other hand, she had no authority in the Mistari main camps unless he acknowledged her.

With her father's blessing, she would be able to contact the leaders of the Mistari and try to find a tribe that would take in Jeht and Quean. A tribe that *didn't* revolve around bloodshed and brute force. At the same time, if she could find the courage to face him, she could remove the looming ax of terror that threatened to fall on her at the simplest mention of someone like Christian Denmark.

"I will wait, if you think it best," Jeht said.

He did not say how long.

Bolstering her courage by telling herself she was doing the right thing, Sarik left Jeht with his brother, and then returned to the administration building and picked up one of the disposable cell phones kept on hand for residents who did not want to be found. She wasn't going to give her father a chance to track her down until she was sure he was going to follow the laws.

It has been six years. You were sixteen when you saw him last, she told herself as she punched in the numbers with trembling hands. She never wanted to see him again, never wanted him in her life. But was she so much of a coward that she couldn't call him, even if it meant Jeht and Quean would someday have a home again?

She sat in her car to make the phone call so she would not risk anyone walking up and greeting her or saying anything that might tip her father off about where she was. She wrapped herself in noble motives and precautions, but the instant she heard his voice on the phone, she felt like she was standing before him again, looking up at him, powerless and frightened.

"*Divai*, Father," she said, her voice barely a whisper.

There was a pause before he replied to the greeting. "*La'he'gen-ne'rai.*" The response was as formal as her own words. He greeted her as daughter, though his tone was cautious. And immediately, he asked, "Where are you?"

"I won't tell you that yet." It was so hard to say those words. "I need you to—"

"Is someone holding you against your will?" he interrupted. She tried to answer, to tell him no, but he spoke over her. "If they are, if *anyone* has put a hand on you to hurt you, I will—"

"I need you to *listen* to me!" she shouted, barely able to hear her voice over her own pulse.

"I need you to tell me where you are," he replied.

She hung up, her heart pounding in her throat.

She was crazy to have tried.

Stupid.

She dismantled the phone with shaking fingers and crushed the delicate machinery, leaving nothing for him to trace. He might have cared about the cubs in other circumstances, but he wouldn't listen to anything Sarik had to say until he had her back in his possession. Was it her responsibility to sacrifice her own life and freedom just to explore the possibility that her father might be willing to help?

Not wanting to risk running into Christian, she returned to her room instead of going to the children with yet more frustrating news. Jeht needed some time to process what she had told him, and she needed to wait until she had shut her panic down before she faced him again.

When Jason found her, she was calmly checking messages and emails. She had been networking for days, trying to make contact with *someone* who might have ties to the Mistari main camps. Her mailbox was full of apologies and dismissals.

"How's it going with the cubs?" Jason asked, looking over her shoulder at the latest email, with its hostile message: *How could you want to send children back to that barbaric culture?*

Unfortunately, individuals who had willingly left the Mistari tended not to have a high opinion of their ways.

"Not well," she admitted. "Jeht and Quean don't understand why someone would willingly leave, or why I would choose not to go back, so it's hard to explain why I haven't found a way to get them home yet."

"Yeah," Jason said, his gaze distant. "I remember what that's like."

Jason had saved Sarik's life, after she had stupidly walked into his master's territory when she was sixteen. After they first ran away, they had clung together not out of any affection, but because neither of them knew how to survive without someone to fight—and they had fought, brutally, physically, and verbally, time and again, until they realized they were echoing everything they had been taught and wanted to get away from. They had joined SingleEarth with no real expectation of finding anything there for them, but they hadn't known anywhere else to go.

Sarik hadn't spoken to her father since, before today. He

wasn't the type who would be proud of her work at Single-Earth. He would be disgusted and order her home immediately, and if she refused, he would exert his significant physical and political power to get what he wanted. There was no relationship she could maintain with him in which she was not a terrified subject under his rule—which meant it was better if he never knew where she was.

CHAPTER 9

THOUGH CHRISTIAN WORE his detached-and-bored expression during most of Lynzi's "tour," Alysia could tell he was intrigued by the shooting. Had it been intended to warn Alysia, scare her, draw her out, or drive her away? Given that her own weapons had been used, someone was probably planning to frame her, but who would hate her enough to want to implicate her, have the talent to make the shots, and yet care enough to avoid any kills? And where was the follow-through, the pointed finger directing blame her way?

She wished she could discuss all the possibilities with Christian.

They found Ben camped out in the cafeteria, swearing at a laptop.

"I thought you were heading home," Alysia said.

"I am. Will be," Ben answered. "I'm waiting for the IT monkeys to show up so I can tell them what's going on. We've got a root kit to clean up, and probably about a dozen computers that need to be quarantined, formatted, and reimaged. Maybe more. They're going to have to rebuild the entire network."

"Glad I'm not on that job," Alysia admitted. "How did you get out of doing it?"

"I offered to nuke it from orbit," Ben answered. "Central said they'd send in a cleanup crew. I got *shot*, remember? Hey, is this the big, bad mercenary the guards are all on edge about?" he asked, looking up at Christian. "Did you want to know more about this critter? As best as I can tell, it came in as a fraudulent update. Added itself to the security suite's whitelist and then downloaded a handful of patches so it could—"

Christian shook his head, cutting Ben off with a, "Thanks. I already have the information I need."

Alysia had explained that a computer virus had been planted and how it had an impact on everyone's movements that morning; that was as much as Christian wanted to know. His eyes had glazed over when Ben started talking root kits and patches.

"You're really leader of Frost now?" Alysia found herself asking as they moved on.

She didn't care if Lynzi heard the question. Watching Christian with Ben had offended her in a visceral way.

Of the three Bruja guilds, Frost had traditionally been

the stereotypical redneck cousin, specializing in hand-to-hand combat and brute force without the finesse or standards of Crimson or Onyx. Alysia, however, had spent most of her time in Bruja trying to convince the guilds that they needed to move into the twenty-first century, a notion that had terrified most of the old-guard leadership. As a result, Frost was now the most technologically advanced of the guilds—or had been before she left, before a hunter who didn't know a monitor from a microwave took over.

She was appropriately chastised as Christian replied, "Someone needed to take it after Sarta left." He didn't say the rest aloud, which was *And you weren't there.*

"What does leadership mean in a group like Bruja?" Lynzi asked. "Would the leader of Onyx have the authority to order members to stay away from us, if we could make it worth his while to do so?"

Christian shook his head. "Kral wouldn't make that deal, and he wouldn't be able to enforce it if he did. Leaders are responsible for intervening if the guild's reputation is threatened or if we are exposed to the wrong people, not for policing the actions of individual members. Not so different from a Haven mediator, in a way," he added, with a pointed look to Alysia.

"I think SingleEarth's response to a threat is probably subtler than Bruja's," Lynzi observed.

There was little further conversation as Lynzi showed them around the area and then led them back to Christian's car, where she asked, "Do you have any thoughts?"

"Not yet," Christian answered, "but I know how to contact you if I need to."

Lynzi nodded. "This Haven has been my home for forty years. I have three circles of power around it, and you do not have nearly the control to veil yourself sufficiently to cross those circles without my feeling it. Are we clear?"

"Clear," he answered.

Alysia asked, "Can you feel him because he's another Triste, or can you sense everyone who comes and goes?"

"I can sense everyone," Lynzi answered, understanding why Alysia asked, "but I don't normally pay attention unless I feel another Triste or someone unusually powerful. I didn't feel anything noteworthy before the attack."

"Interesting," Christian commented, then turned to Alysia. "I'll stay in town today. If there's another attack, or if you just want to talk without a babysitter around, you'll be able to find me." He looked back at the other Triste. "Lynzi," he said, and offered his hand, which she shook. "Happy hunting."

Alysia waited until Christian's taillights faded in the distance before saying to Lynzi, "So what now?"

Lynzi gave her a long, measured look, before asking, "Are you still in Bruja?"

"No." No matter what doubts and questions Christian had put into her head, Alysia found herself thoroughly glad to be able to answer the question honestly. She suspected that Lynzi would know if she were lying.

"Do you know who shot us?"

"No."

"As long as you're living here peacefully and honestly, you are welcome to stay," Lynzi said. "You are also free to leave, if you want. But if you choose to stay here and you bring bloodshed into my home, then I will need to respond. Is that clear?"

"Yes," Alysia answered around the hitch in her throat.

"Let me know if you and Christian come up with any theories. But you should probably let him sleep a couple hours before you visit him. He's exhausted."

"Remind me never to underestimate you," Alysia said, resisting the urge to step back from the witch.

Lynzi smiled and said, "I think I just did. Now, I'm going to go back to bed until a decent hour of the day. Take care, Alysia."

"Yeah. Take care."

Unsure what else to do, Alysia returned to her room. What next? Did she want to track Christian down? She needed to, if she wanted to solve the riddle of this attack before someone else was hurt, but she wasn't sure she was ready to face him without her so-called babysitter.

A knock pulled her from her spinning thoughts.

"Yeah?" She approached the door to peer through the peephole, and saw Ben leaning against the far wall.

"Do you have a minute?" he asked. "I'm trying to get this virus cleaned up so I can get the hell out of here, but I could use a second opinion on the code."

She reached for the doorknob and then hesitated, feeling some old instinct kick her in the shins. "I can probably help you out, but how did you know to come to me?"

Through the peephole, she watched Ben's face fall. His

tone stayed mostly upbeat, but his expression was crestfallen as he said, "We worked together on the Mahoney issue a few months back. Just that once, though, so no big deal you don't remember me."

She remembered the job, which had been ten times as difficult as it should have been because SingleEarth seemed to think it would go faster if they assigned as many techs as possible. She had been too busy being angry at everyone else working with her to bother to remember their names or faces.

"Right, of course," she said as she opened the door. "Come on in. You can set your computer up anywhere," she added when she realized he was carrying a laptop bag.

As he reached into it, she hesitated again; her body tensed for no obvious reason except that some part of her brain was expecting something more dangerous than a computer to come out of the beat-up black bag.

Ben wasn't a threat; he was even still limping, as the muscles in his thigh continued to knit themselves together. And Christian had looked right at him without recognition.

"It'll just take me a minute to load this," Ben said. "Don't suppose you have a Coke or something I can steal?"

Geeks and caffeine, Alysia thought, with some humor. "I wish," she answered. "I haven't had a chance to stock the fridge since I got here."

"I wonder what got in the way," Ben said, so dryly she wasn't completely sure he had intended sarcasm. He looked back at the computer screen and opened a file. "Here, come look at this."

She had put half the room between them, but now she

leaned in to check out the code he had brought up in a text file. At first glance, it seemed like a nasty little computer virus.

"Here, sit," Ben said. "It's a beast, complicated as hell. Mind if I get myself some water?"

"Go ahead." Some people could recognize handwriting; Alysia could recognize a programmer by his code, and she was sure she had seen this style before. She scrolled through, trying to get a sense of what the virus had been intended to do, and why the style seemed so familiar.

"I have a couple questions," Ben said as he stepped into the kitchen.

"Yeah?" she asked, without looking up from the screen.

A jolt made her nearly jump out of her skin at the same time that her chair toppled backward. Her effort to catch herself was sabotaged by a sneakered foot knocking her arm out of the way, so she landed awkwardly, at the same time that Ben asked, "Question one is, why'd you shoot me?"

Strangely, the first emotion she felt once her vision cleared and she could focus on Ben standing above her with a punch-dagger in his hand was relief. Her instincts weren't completely dead.

She might be, though.

"I didn't shoot you," she said. "What were you doing here that I should have shot you for?"

"I'm willing to believe you, but only because you let me get behind you just now," Ben said. "But seriously, don't get up," he added when she started to shift position to do just that. "Question two is, why is someone offering a half-million dollars for the delivery of your still-breathing body?"

"News to me," she answered. She had been debating how it would go if she tried to cut his legs out from under him, but if he was hoping to take her alive, she could take more time considering her strategy. She was out of shape, which meant that any way she fought back had to be fast and dirty. "Are you Crimson?"

Onyx members rarely went undercover, but Christian hadn't even blinked to see this guy in the hall, which meant he wasn't from Frost.

"That's your gig, babe," Ben answered. He knelt down near her, close enough that he was either very stupid or very certain of his ability to defend himself. "Within the history of the Bruja guilds, maybe a dozen members have gone multiclass. I can count on one hand the number of members who have reached third rank in all three guilds. I can count on one finger the number of folks who reached third rank and then had the spine to tell the leadership to go to hell."

She shifted position again, slowly. When he didn't tell her to stop, she moved inch by inch until she was sitting against the wall. "I can't tell if you're flirting or trying to kidnap me," she remarked, noting that he had sidestepped her question in favor of sharing his observations about her.

"I don't do captures," Ben answered.

"Did you plant the computer virus?" He seemed to have stopped immediately threatening her, but he hadn't put down the knife.

"Duh," he answered. "All I needed to do was intercept the call to tech support and I had an excuse to come look you up. Most of us figured you were rotting in a ditch somewhere, you see, but then you showed up on CNN. Are you by any chance here stalking an Onyx creep with lousy aim? Because if so, I want in."

She shook her head. "I wasn't stalking anyone until they attacked me. Was the number against me up before the shooting?" She had been so distracted by Christian that she had never taken a good look at the job board at the Onyx guild hall. Had her name been on it?

Ben shook his head. "It just flashed a half hour ago, listing SE Haven Number Four as your location. Hidden client, private posting to all three guilds."

"If it only happened a half hour ago, then how did you hear about it?" He hadn't been to any of the guild halls where he might have picked up a message; she was sure of that.

"There's an app for that," Ben answered, once again completely straight-faced. "The question is, when will Christian hear about it, and do you think he'll call?"

She couldn't tell if he was being honest or just screwing with her. It didn't really matter, as long as he wasn't trying to kill or kidnap her. "Fine. Thanks for the heads-up, but I want you gone. Now, or I'm going to have to try to make you gone."

He grinned. "You'd lose."

Alysia shrugged. "It's the principle of the thing."

She jumped when he leaned in to her, just long enough to kiss her cheek. "That's what I love about you, babe," he said as he pushed to his feet, all evidence of a limp gone. "You have the wackiest principles I know. And yeah, I'm out of here." He quickly packed the laptop back into its case. "I suggest you get out, too."

He had closed the door behind him before Alysia was able to push herself to her feet. Her heart was pounding in her throat, and insanely, it felt *good*. She was unarmed, SingleEarth still had some kind of Onyx stalker on the loose, and now someone was offering a very large amount of money to anyone willing to try to abduct her.

She hadn't felt so alive in two years.

CHAPTER 10

IT WAS HER fifth birthday, and her father had brought her out to a fancy party. She wore a pretty dress and a shiny necklace, and her hair had been put up special with a glittering gold clip shaped like a butterfly.

There were metal detectors and guards at the door. Her father's cuff links set off the detectors, and the guards made him remove his tuxedo jacket so they could search him thoroughly. Her butterfly made the machines beep, too, but they let her pass.

The party was beautiful, full of dancing people who oohed and aahed over her. Isn't she lovely? So poised. So sweet. *None of them knew there was a dagger hidden in her hair, under the pretty butterfly her father had known would set off the metal detectors.*

Her father asked for the knife about half an hour after they ar-
rived. They left shortly after, amid the screaming. He bought her a
cupcake at a restaurant on the way home, wished her happy birthday,
and thanked her for being a good girl and making him proud.

There was blood on her fancy big-girl shoes. She kicked them off
under the table and walked barefoot back to the car. Her father didn't
notice. He never noticed things like that.

Sarik woke with a start, disoriented and sore. The move
sent a long-cold coffee sloshing over its rim onto the desk.

She had intended to close her eyes for just a moment. Just
a second. She had been on edge for days, her sleep mocked by
memories surfacing as nightmares.

It wasn't even eleven in the morning, and Jason was still
sleeping in the next room. The worst part was, she had been
happy that day, deliriously pleased, because her father had
made time to celebrate her birthday and because she had made
him proud. She hadn't understood that she had been there
only because she was useful.

As she grew up, it all became harder. Every moment became a power struggle, an impossible balance, as her father
groomed her to be his heir, always demanding perfect obedi-
ence. Warning her that she needed to be strong and then beating her so badly she couldn't walk if she dared try to turn that
strength against him.

She jumped when hands descended on her shoulders.

"Sorry," Jason said. "I said your name, but you were a million miles away."

"Sorry," she echoed, pulling away as she stood up.

I can't do this anymore. If she had to keep running, hiding, doing anything in her power to try to stifle the fear, it was going to destroy her.

"Sarik," Jason said softly, "I know we've had this conversation before, so I won't push it, but . . . well, one of the counselors came to me after the attack, to see if I wanted to schedule a time to talk. I think it could be a good idea for you, too."

"I wasn't hurt," she replied. *Jason* could have been killed, *really* killed.

"Not physically, but—" He broke off, as if he was going to drop it, then decided to forge ahead. "The last time I felt that kind of pain or had blood on my skin was in Maya's cell the day I met you."

The day I met you. He didn't understand how those words sounded in her ears, not like the empathy he intended but like accusation.

"I'm sure this attack has dredged up just as many traumatic memories for you as it has for me. There's no shame in needing some help to—"

"No," she interrupted. "If you want to talk to someone, I'll love you and support you and hope they can help. But it's not for me."

He looked like he wanted to argue once more but said only, "I need to feed, and then I'm going to call Diana. Maya is powerful, but she is still only one mercenary. She wouldn't dare challenge SingleEarth openly." He looked away as he added, "But she might send someone to harass us anonymously, if she thought it could scare me away from here and back to her. I'm going to tell Diana everything and let her decide what to do next."

The words seemed to place a clamp around Sarik's throat. She wanted to say *You don't need to do that,* but she couldn't.

Jason kissed her cheek. "I love you, Sarik."

"I love you," she whispered, but only after he was out the door.

Alysia. It wasn't too late. Sarik could still make this right. She just needed to talk to the table's newest mediator and explain everything. *Everything,* down to the moment when she had peeked inside the trunk in the human's room, found enough weapons to arm a half-dozen killers, and been sure down to her toes that Alysia was here to finish what Maya's brood had failed to do six years earlier.

Jason didn't understand, because Sarik had never told him who Cori was.

For a long time, Sarik had been too afraid to admit anything to Jason. He had been a mercenary, after all; she didn't want him to realize she could be valuable to anyone. He hadn't made the connection between the dead girl and Sarik because he had no reason to assume there *could* be any relationship between a runaway tiger of pure royal blood and a human child.

By the time she trusted him enough to tell him, she was already someone else, and Sarik kuloka Mari had slammed the door on her painful past.

So now, only she had the information necessary to know that the recent bloodshed wasn't about Jason. It was about Bruja, about Alysia.

Alysia, who had stepped forward to help when the attack happened. Who had been alone with Sarik for hours when they went to Onyx but hadn't made a single move to threaten her. Who just maybe wasn't the villian Sarik had thought she was but instead was hiding from the same demons Sarik was trying to dodge.

Sarik couldn't talk to a counselor. Couldn't explain to Diana without putting all of SingleEarth in danger. Couldn't even really explain to Jason. But if she had the courage, she could tell Alysia, and they could work out what needed to happen next.

Her mind was full of white noise as she crossed the hall in search of the human mediator. As she knocked, though, the door swung open.

The trunk was open, and most of its contents had been dumped onto the bed. The weapons were gone, as was Alysia's laptop. Sarik couldn't tell if anything else was missing, except for Alysia herself. The question was, had she left willingly or been taken?

Sarik hurried to the parking lot to see if Alysia's car was there, and found her in the process of opening the driver's-side door. She was carrying a backpack, as well as a black case slung over the same shoulder. And someone stood between them, watching his prey.

Alysia was being stalked.

The vampire glanced to the side in response to a door closing at one of the nearby buildings, and Sarik caught a glimpse of the red teardrop decorating his left earlobe.

She recognized the symbol. Jason had an identical piece

of jewelry still tucked at the back of his drawer, wrapped in a scrap of fabric. He had worn it for almost a year after he had left Maya, as if it were a symbol of that bit of her he couldn't quite rip from himself.

Sarik could have called a warning, but Alysia did not have a weapon in her hand.

Bracing herself mentally, she let her vision narrow to a point at the back of the vampire's spine. She leaned forward, putting her hands on the hood of the nearest car. As she boosted herself up, she shifted shape, so it was a tiger's paw that landed on the back bumper and a full-grown tiger who bounded over the car and then stretched in an arc, leaping with a roar. By the time the vampire turned, she was already on top of him.

Alysia turned at the sound of the tiger's weight driving the vampire to the ground, her eyes going wide as the tiger roared and, with one quick shake, broke the vampire's neck.

Sarik stumbled back, spitting out the too-familiar taste of blood in her mouth, fighting nausea and overwhelming sense-memory. She reverted to human form, seeking a human's dulled senses.

"Thanks," Alysia said, sounding dazed. She knelt by the vampire's side and reached out to tilt his head so she could get a better look at the earring. "He's a mercenary," she said, probably assuming Sarik wouldn't already know that. She drew a slender knife from a makeshift holster at her waist. "I don't know exactly who's after me, but it's me they're after," she said. "So I'm leaving. I'm not pitting SingleEarth against the Bruja guilds, not over me. SingleEarth isn't weak, but Bruja—"

"Don't," Sarik protested as she realized Alysia intended to drive the knife into the vampire's heart. "He ..." She trailed off.

The human hesitated and said, "His spine will heal in less than a minute. He was sent to kidnap me, but he'll want to kill you for hurting him. You do not want him getting back up."

Sarik didn't want him getting back up, but she also didn't want him dead. A few years earlier, it might have been Jason lying there. The ones who had seen Sarik, who might recognize her, were all dead. But Alysia was right—he wasn't going to get up and just forgive her for breaking his neck.

Alysia moved to drive the knife down, not waiting for any more objections from Sarik, but the hesitation was costly. The vampire jerked his arm, the movement not smooth but sufficient to divert the blade from his heart so it only grazed his opposite shoulder. Even so, he hissed in pain, and Sarik caught the acrid smell of firestone touching vampiric blood.

The vampire threw Alysia to the side and snatched the blade Alysia had tried to end him with.

Move. Help them.

She didn't know how to help Alysia without getting in the way.

A black and golden blur shot past her. It was smaller than her own tiger form, immature, but fearless as it leapt into the fray, first on paws and then coalescing into the form of a young boy who was small and lithe enough to put himself between the two combatants, carrying his own knife.

"Jeht!" Sarik shrieked, running forward. He must have

heard her roar, an instinctive sound of fury that could be heard for miles around.

The fight was over in another instant as the triumphant nine-year-old let out a hoot and turned to Sarik with blood on his hands and a dagger in his fist.

Alysia scrambled back from the vampire's corpse and the exultant child. "You all right, kid?" Alysia asked as she snatched the firestone knife off the ground.

Jeht didn't answer her but hurried back to Sarik's side, looking proud. He had defended his territory, killed an intruder. He hadn't hesitated like Sarik had.

"You hurt him," Jeht said. "He would have wanted to kill you. You can't let people live who want to kill you."

That's why you're here, Sarik wanted to say. *Because your tribe had the same twisted principles that my father's has, and the new leader knew you would try to kill him for killing your father.*

She said, "Jeht, it's more complicated than that."

"Are more coming?" he asked.

Sarik looked up at Alysia, who was leaning against the side of her car, staring at Jeht as if he had grown a second head. She said, "Tell me you'll get that kid some therapy." She opened her car door. "And thank him for helping me out. And let Lynzi know I didn't mean to bring this down on you all. Really, I didn't. I won't be back before I sort it out."

She tossed her backpack and the weapons case onto the passenger seat and closed the door without another word. As Sarik watched Alysia drive away, she said to Jeht, "Give me the knife."

He handed her the weapon, which looked like it had been made with sharpened flatware from the cafeteria. As she took it, she realized there was blood on her hands as well.

"Let's go clean up," she said.

It's over. Not the way she wanted it to be over, but what else could she do?

CHAPTER 11

CHRISTIAN WAS STILL sleeping when he heard a knock on his hotel room door. He opened his eyes, shut them against the glare of midday sun streaming in his window, and then forced them open once more as he stood up and crossed to the door.

Before he reached it or leaned down to look through the peephole, Alysia said, "It's me. Can I come in?"

He couldn't help but smile. He hadn't told her where he was staying, or even the name he had used to register at this hotel, but he had used a name she would recognize from past exploits. It had probably taken Alysia ten minutes, at most, to hack into and scan through local hotel registries in order to track him down.

Christian remembered the day that Alysia had tried to

explain to him why she had worked so hard to digitalize Frost, and why the Bruja guilds needed to move "out of the Stone Age and into the Silicon Age." *Piracy isn't done with a ship and a sword anymore*, she had told him, pacing back and forth, frustrated by his lack of interest. *A Crimson or Onyx member might take a contract to kill some wealthy businessman, probably because his heirs want to inherit his money, but it ends there. In the digital world, it's possible to assassinate a man's character, steal his identity, turn his world upside down without ever spilling a drop of blood. Bruja was big and powerful two centuries ago, but these days, they're earning penny candy to engage in little local scuffles. They're going to fade into obscurity if they don't realize the world has upgraded from a blade to binary.*

Christian didn't understand half the words Alysia used when she went on one of her tech rants—Onyx had never been big on computer work, so he knew little about them—but her passion on the subject never failed to make him grin, especially when it made the leaders of Crimson, Onyx, and the Bruja guilds gnash their teeth because they knew she was right but refused to admit it.

His smile disappeared when he opened the door and saw the blood on her face. She glanced over her shoulder as he pulled her inside, and that was enough warning for him to shut, lock, and bolt the door behind her.

"Someone following you?" he asked, his eyes lingering on a cut down her cheek. It was too neat to be the result of someone's fist splitting the skin; that wound had been made by a blade.

"Could be," she answered. "You haven't heard?"

"Heard what?" She flinched as he reached toward the

wound, which had started to scab in places but was still seeping blood in others. "How badly are you hurt?"

"Not too bad," she said. "If you have bandages—"

"I have better," he replied, gently brushing his fingertips over the edges of the wound. The lingering aura of firestone told him why the injury wasn't worse: firestone drained vampiric power and wasn't too good for shapeshifters, but it was less dangerous for humans than pure steel would be. The witch power embedded in the stone had helped her body staunch the bleeding.

Alysia stayed tensed, but she didn't pull away again as he focused his power on the way her flesh had been cut and gently nudged it back into its proper form. If it hadn't been on her face, he might have stopped as soon as the wound was closed, but he didn't want to leave a scar, so he put a little extra power into erasing all evidence of the blade.

Alysia wasn't vain, but scars drew attention. They looked suspicious.

Plus, he didn't want to leave a mark on her face. But he knew she would accept the first explanation more than the second one. "Anything else?" he asked.

"Some bruised ribs," she answered, "but that's all. It could have been a lot worse. There's a number up for my capture, apparently."

"Since when?" he asked. He had checked all three guild boards before meeting Alysia that morning, to confirm that there wasn't anything up about an attack on SingleEarth. He would have noticed a posting calling for Alysia's abduction.

"Since about an hour ago, according to Ben," she said. "It

even included my location. Someone probably called him because he was already there."

"Ben the computer guy?" Christian asked. He had looked
the geek in the eye and hadn't seen or sensed a thing. Of
course, he hadn't spent a lot of time at Crimson since Alysia
left—he had watched their Challenge because he wanted to
know who Adam's successor would be, but he hadn't even
competed—so it was possible Ben was a recent member of that
guild. "*He* did this to you?"

"No, he's the one who gave me the heads-up. He doesn't
do live captures," she answered. The explanation wasn't hard
to believe; a lot of the mercenaries in Bruja would happily kill
someone but had no interest in the inconvenience of a living
prisoner. Especially in Crimson, it was rare to find someone
interested in accepting a job for a capture.

Still, there were enough people who *would* go for a well-
paying capture that it would be a good idea to move on as
soon as possible. Christian had specifically chosen his current
location so that Alysia could find him. If she could, so could
others.

He reached forward again, intending to check on her ribs,
but Alysia flinched again.

"One of Maya's grunts gave me the new decorations," she
said, not meeting his gaze. "Unless she's changed her ways
and is giving her boys free will these days, that means more
of them will show up soon. I have my rank-weapons, but no
good way to carry most of them. Plus, I'm out of shape. I've
had two people get the drop on me in less than an hour, and I
think I got rescued by a nine-year-old."

Normally Christian would have laughed and asked for the rest of that story, but Alysia's jovial tone was too forced.

He hadn't been a Triste the last time they had hunted together, so it was possible that the chaotic splash of emotions in her aura was normal for her when she was amped up for a fight, but he doubted it. One thing he knew for sure was that there were streaks of pain in there as well, pulsing in time with her breathing.

"Do you want me to check the ribs?" he asked.

Alysia paused, regarding him warily as she asked, "How much power do you burn with that kind of healing?"

"Not enough to compromise my ability to fight if we get in trouble," he answered.

She didn't answer immediately, and in the silence, the truth hit him. Alysia had left before he started training. The kind of ground rules they had set in the old days didn't address situations in which one of them was potentially prey for the other.

"If I ever feed on you," Christian assured her, "it will be because I need to in order to keep us alive, and I will make very sure you know about it. You trust me more than is normally healthy in our profession, but if I violated that trust by feeding on you, I have absolutely no doubt you would do everything in your power to kill me. Am I right?"

"Yeah." She cautiously prodded her ribs, her gaze distant. "Nothing's cracked. I'll be fine, if I can figure out who's offering a half-million dollars to kidnap me. It seems unlikely they just want to throw a surprise party."

It has been two years, he reminded himself. They were both pretending no time had passed, but Alysia's aura held the twisted shine of panic or even shock. Even if he had read her correctly earlier, even if she did miss Bruja—and, hopefully, him—she wasn't here of her own free will. She was here because she had nowhere else to go.

But she trusts me enough to come here, to let me know I could earn a lot of quick cash for bringing her in, and to admit that she probably wouldn't be able to defend herself. She had trusted him enough to let her guard down the instant she recognized him that morning at SingleEarth, too. That meant something, right?

"Let's move while we talk," he said. "We can go by the house, get you better equipped, and then I can look up the posting against you."

Alysia nodded. "Lead the way."

"Could it be someone *at* SingleEarth who has it in for you?" Christian asked as he set a hand to the door and focused his power, checking the hall for any sign of movement. "Or did anyone else know where you were?"

"I take it you haven't started watching the news in my absence," Alysia remarked, following as he stepped through the door.

Her hand once again drifted to her cheek. Did it feel strange? He probably should have asked before healing it. But he wouldn't have asked before helping her with a bandage. This was no different, really. Except that it obviously was, to her, and despite his assurances, Alysia had put plenty of space between them.

"What was on the news?" he asked.

"Me. And it was national, so the list of people who potentially know where I am isn't short."

They both instinctively quieted as they reached the parking lot. The snow had stopped, and there were people milling about, but it wasn't the possibility of being overheard that made Christian tense. They were too exposed.

"We can leave my car," Alysia said. "It doesn't have anything in it except a completely legal registration under the surname I'm using at SingleEarth."

"Good."

They didn't speak much more until they had both climbed into his car, a nondescript four-wheel drive—the only two things he much cared about when shopping for a vehicle—and Christian brought them out of town and onto what passed for a highway in this backwater spot.

"Question," Alysia said as they left behind most signs of civilization. "Bruja allows contracts against anyone, for any reason, *except* guild leaders. There's no reason I can think of that someone would want me this badly, but what about you? A capture is up close and has a high likelihood of complications compared to a kill, and much as I hate to admit it, there are a lot of people in Bruja who could have predicted I would go to you in this kind of situation. Do you think someone could be hoping you might get caught in the cross fire?"

The suggestion was not beyond the realm of possibility. Even if Christian hadn't been a guild leader, most people would not have wanted to cross Pandora by directly targeting her most recent student. On the other hand, those same

people would know that a Triste was hard to kill and was unlikely to fall accidentally during a job with another purpose.

"It's—"

The silver SUV cut into his field of vision and forced him
to swing left. He heard Alysia yelp an expletive just before
he felt the double concussion of tires exploding. Despite his
Triste reflexes on the wheel, two flat tires on the still-slick
roads sent the car into a spin.

Before he could even panic, the nose of the car was in the
ditch between the road and a state forest.

"Cute," Christian said dryly as he hastily removed his seat
belt and exited the vehicle. Alysia did the same. Neither of
them was stupid enough to believe this had been an accident,
even before Alysia knelt down and picked up one of the silver
stars that had been strewn at the edge of the road, waiting to
destroy any tire that crossed them.

Alysia swore loudly, one hand instinctively going to her
chest as the tension caused a twinge in her bruised ribs, the
other reaching into her backpack, Christian hoped for a knife.
Apparently, she had kept the weapons—probably for their
sentimental value—but hadn't kept easily replaced things like
concealable sheaths on hand.

He drew his own knife and stretched out his awareness,
trying to sense for anything alive or undead nearby. No one
had gone to this much trouble to cause the accident without
having a trap ready to close on them.

"We need to get away from the road," Alysia said. "This
is too exposed. Good Samaritan, EMT, police, tow company,
anyone could pull over and we wouldn't know if they were

for real or the next part of this trap. Can Triste power keep us from freezing to death if we go hiking?"

He didn't get a chance to answer before two more of Maya's crew showed up. Like wild dogs, they tended to travel in packs. Two years earlier, he would have put Alysia at his back and they could easily have taken down a half dozen of Maya's boys, but she was out of practice, and if Alysia was the target, Christian didn't want to put her directly in the vamps' line of sight.

While he was looking over his shoulder to check the situation on her side, however, he missed the appearance of the third vampire. He barely caught a glimpse of the crossbow aimed at him before the bolt hit him high in the right side of the chest.

Perversely, Pandora's training meant he could feel the exact damage done to the soft tissue of his lung, could feel where the edge of a barbed bolt nicked the aorta, a killing injury to almost anyone else.

It took the wind out of his lungs, made him fall, forced him to turn his attention inward to keep his body from bleeding to death.

Alysia will have to hold her own.

CHAPTER 12

TIME AND EVENTS seemed to blur. The fight with the vampire, Alysia, and then Jeht had taken less than a minute, but it seemed to stretch into an hour in Sarik's memory.

In comparison, all the rest happened in a blink. The hunters arrived. Mark the groundskeeper came running after Quean, who had followed Jeht. The man took a child's fist to the mouth as he tried to pull Quean away from the bloody scene.

Lynzi ran up next. She started to kneel to check Jeht for wounds, but Sarik shook her head. He was fine. He ordered Quean to calm down. The younger tiger obediently relaxed in Mark's arms and, sucking his thumb, looked as innocent as any four-year-old.

Jason arrived, but when he first reached for Sarik, she recoiled.

The copper-rot taste of blood was still thick in Sarik's mouth, but the fluid itself had gone dry, leaving a sticky, ashy texture like talcum powder on her tongue. She had more blood on her hands from the knife Jeht had handed her. She couldn't stand for Jason to touch her.

He knelt beside the body instead and told them all, "His name is Liam. He works for a mercenary named Maya. He—"

"He was after Alysia," Sarik said before Jason could blame himself. "I *saw* him stalking her. I needed to warn her. Alysia said this is about her. She says she didn't mean to bring danger here. She's leaving until it's sorted out. She's gone now."

"Sarik, I think you should come inside and sit down," Lynzi said. "You're in shock."

"We can clean this up," one of the hunters offered.

Lynzi nodded to them and ushered all the rest inside to the conference room in the administration building.

Jeht and Quean wouldn't leave Sarik's side, insisting on sitting on the floor next to her chair.

Jeht seemed to have decided that he was her protector. He accepted her as a figure with authority over him only because she was Mistari, an adult queen, and he had seen others at SingleEarth defer to her due to her position as a mediator. He seemed to have decided that, if he could not return to the Mistari homeland, he would create his world here instead, and sit by her side as her enforcer. Quean simply watched, wide-eyed, taking his lead from Sarik and Jeht but never even asking what had happened. Blood was nothing new to him.

Sarik wished they could visit one of the tribes that ran more peacefully so that the boys could see that it *was* possible to live without violence. It was unlikely that any such tribe would be willing to welcome him into their midst—Jeht especially was too much of a threat, a miniature prince who had been raised as a warrior—but seeing how such tribes existed might make him realize that there was value in something other than brute strength.

"Sarik?" People had been talking to her while her mind was so far away.

"Sorry," she said, trying to focus. "I'm being stupid. I wasn't even the one who was attacked. I shouldn't be this disturbed."

It was the taste of blood in her mouth that had done it. That, and Jeht's smile after he'd made the kill. She remembered what that childlike pride felt like.

"That's your father talking, not you," Jason whispered to her. He sat beside her and took one of her hands in both of his. "You shouted to warn Alysia, right?"

"I attacked the vampire," she admitted. "I saw the earring. Recognized it. I knew shouting would warn both of them. I didn't know who would win, so I didn't give him a chance to hurt her. Or to run."

"Thank God you didn't," Jason answered. "Liam wouldn't have dared return to Maya without having accomplished his mission. If you had shouted, he would have fought. You did the right thing."

"Was I still doing the right thing when I told Alysia

to stop?" she snapped. "When she was about to kill him, I froze. Jeht is the one who threw himself into the fight without hesitation."

"If my impression is correct, Alysia is a trained fighter," Lynzi said, joining the conversation. "So is Jeht, as much as we hate in our culture to admit such a thing about a child. You're not, Sarik. Never be ashamed that your instinct doesn't tell you to go for the kill."

I used to be a fighter, Sarik thought. *Now I'm just a victim who needs to be protected.*

No, not a victim, she corrected herself. *A survivor. Pull it together, Sarik.*

She took a deep breath and looked up. She could tell that Jeht, sitting near her feet, had sensed her drawing up her strength. He sat a little straighter.

"I know you're still shaken," Lynzi said from across the room, "but if you're ready, we need to know exactly what happened. We cannot afford to assume that Alysia was the only target or that these attacks will stop just because she left. I have been doing research into the Bruja guilds since the first attack, and, well, let's just say I hope we can avoid a direct conflict."

The words echoed something Alysia had said: *I'm not pitting SingleEarth against the Bruja guilds, not over me. SingleEarth isn't weak, but—*

Sarik had interrupted Alysia there, but she knew what the rest would have been: *Neither is Bruja.* And Bruja had more trained, ruthless mercenaries.

In as much detail as she could manage, Sarik recounted everything she had seen, from the moment she noticed the vampire behind Alysia in the parking lot to when everyone else started to arrive.

Jason supplemented the story with what he knew about Maya. "She specializes in captures—kidnapping, extortion, that sort of thing," he said. "If that's the goal, it would explain why the first attack wasn't meant to be fatal. The Onyx attacker could have followed Alysia when she left her room, then lost track of her in the snow and thought she was with our group. They realized they hadn't hit their target and split, and their employer hired Maya next."

"You said before that Christian has some pretty close ties to the leader of Onyx. If the original shooter was from that guild, he also might have balked once Christian got involved," Lynzi suggested, "so the client probably called in a new mercenary from outside the guilds. This might actually work for us. The Bruja guilds are too powerful for us to go against directly, but if this Maya is an independent mercenary, *she* can probably be bought. Jason, what do you think?"

He nodded. "With SingleEarth's resources, absolutely."

"Then we can—"

They were interrupted by a knock at the door.

"Come in," Lynzi called. For most people, it would have been reckless to call out without even looking through the peephole, but Lynzi's magic would have alerted her if someone approached who was powerful enough to be a threat.

Mary opened the door and peeked her head inside.

"I'm sorry to interrupt," she said, "but I have a young woman in the lobby looking for Alysia. She seems very upset but won't tell me what's going on. Is anyone available to speak to her?"

"Please bring her in," Lynzi said. After the secretary walked away, Lynzi added, "I hope you all have your seat belts buckled. This Haven hasn't even had a chance to adjust to losing Joseph. Losing Alysia after she has barely had a chance to walk in the door is going to put a strain on our residents."

Their guest, who arrived a minute later, was wearing worn blue jeans and a sand-colored peasant blouse. Her hair, which was a rich burgundy color, was pulled back, which put more emphasis on her dark, cinnamon-colored eyes. Sarik found herself staring at the woman, wondering, *What now?*

"Come in," Lynzi said. "What can we do for you?"

"The secretary told me Alysia is gone," the woman said, her eyes wide.

"I'm sorry to say she left SingleEarth just recently," Lynzi answered. "Were you working with her?"

The woman drew a breath and nodded. "My little sister," the woman said. "She's been . . . ill, I guess? Or something? You see, our father left when she was very young. We didn't know he was . . . I'm standing here and I'm sorry but it still sounds crazy. I mean, *shapeshifters? Seriously?*"

"Sarik, why don't you speak to our guest?" Lynzi suggested.

"Who the hell are you, the babysitter?" the newcomer demanded, looking at Sarik and the two boys.

Jeht started to stand when the woman turned on Sarik

with obvious anger, but Sarik put a hand on his shoulder to calm him and tried to explain. "I can—"

"What are you?" their guest asked bluntly.

"I'm a shapeshifter," Sarik answered. "Like your sister."

"You're a snake?"

"No," Sarik answered. "I'm a tiger, actually. But—"

"Then what good are you?" the woman asked waspishly, before dropping her gaze and looking chastised. "I'm sorry. This is all just too much for me." She turned to go, saying, "I'll come back when I can talk to another human being."

She stormed out, not leaving any contact information.

Sarik and the other mediators exchanged glances, and after a few moments, Lynzi said, "That was odd." The Triste frowned, shaking her head before saying, "Well, it *wasn't* odd for this place, but it seemed off somehow."

Sarik didn't attempt to make a judgment on the woman's behavior. She doubted her own could be trusted just then.

"Family members of serpiente who have been raised human tend to go through a particularly difficult process," Lynzi reminded them all. "Seeking help was probably difficult for her—only possible at all because she could convince herself that she could trust another human."

Serpiente were not just shapeshifters; even in human form, their bodies functioned differently from humans'. Among other things, their slow metabolisms made them nearly cold-blooded. When raised human, they tended to start changing during adolescence, a painful process that often triggered many series of tests and hospitalizations before they came to Single-Earth's attention. Family members often had to transition from mourning for a loved one they thought was dying to coping with the knowledge that there was an entire world they had previously thought of as the provenance of myth and campfire stories.

"Should someone go after her?" Sarik asked.

"Chasing her through SingleEarth is not going to make her feel safer," Lynzi replied. "She will either come back on her own or find a human mediator she trusts at another Haven. On the other hand, I think this is a good cue for us to adjourn. Sarik, the cubs could use your attention right now. Jason, stay a moment?"

Sarik nodded, recognizing a dismissal when she heard one, but she looked to Jason instead of leaving immediately. He gave a half smile and said, "I had to face her someday. It's a lot easier to face a mercenary with the weight of the wealthiest organization in the world at your back."

Sarik heard the false bravado in his words, but sometimes that was the only way to face one's fears. *Fake it till you make it,* she thought.

Meanwhile, as Lynzi and Jason discussed how to handle Maya, Sarik had to find a way to explain to the child who had probably saved her life as well as Alysia's that it wasn't nice to kill people.

"Are these people warriors?" Jeht asked after they left the room.

Maybe that was the answer.

"Yes," she said, "but not in the way you think. There are ways to be a leader, and to protect your people, that don't rely on violence and brute strength."

She had been thinking that if the cubs could not return to the Mistari, she needed to convince them that they didn't need to be warriors. That wasn't the right approach. It was too late to convince them that they didn't always need to be ready for battle, but perhaps it wasn't too late to make them see that not every battle involved claws or a blade.

Maybe, along the way, she could finally convince herself of the same thing.

CHAPTER 13

ALYSIA SAW CHRISTIAN go down but couldn't spare any attention to see how badly he was hurt. Tristes were tough to kill—most people weren't crazy enough to try. At that moment, she had to put all her focus on the two vampires who were flanking her.

And then there was one, she thought as Christian reached out and dragged one of them away from her. Judging from the bloodsucker's shriek, Christian used more than his bare hands. Tristes were famous for making vampires their preferred prey, and an injured Triste was probably in no mood to be gentle.

Alysia saw the sniper just past where Christian was grappling with his vampiric target, and managed to throw her opponent in front of the next bolt that came her way. She followed him down with a stake, but the archer reloaded too quickly; before she could get under cover, she felt the impact in her flesh. A steel-and-aluminum shaft shattered her knee-cap on its way to burying its head in that vulnerable joint, sending black pain through her.

She was more aware of shadows and movement than she was of events in the next few seconds while she struggled to breathe, to somehow get her body ready to fight.

She looked up again to find Christian standing, facing the direction where the archer had been a moment ago. The at-tacker must have decided flight was the better part of valor.

Thankfully, he didn't see what Alysia saw, which was Christian stumbling back so he could lean against the car and slide slowly to the ground, gray-faced. The blood on his lips spread further when he tried to talk and ended up coughing instead.

It took all Alysia's willpower to move herself closer and not scream as the bolt in her knee shifted. The distance couldn't have been more than a couple feet, but the move sapped all her energy. By the time she reached Christian, she was fighting nausea and breathing heavily, struggling just to stay conscious.

Don't you dare pass out, she told herself. *You will not wake up in a better place.*

Christian reached over, and the instant his fingertips touched her cheek, the worst of the pain receded. The fluttery sensation in her chest remained, as did the pulse of adrenaline and the bolt that had completely punctured her left knee. Her *good* knee. He had been able to take away her body's reactions, but not the injury itself.

As she examined the bolt high in Christian's chest, she said, "If you were still human, I'd say your only chance with that injury is a damn good witch."

How well could Christian heal these days? How fast? And how well could he fight once he was done? Because the vampire with the crossbow might have run for now, but he would be back, probably with reinforcements.

"Pull it."

At first, Alysia could only stare. "You sure?"

When he nodded, she tried to remind herself that he knew what he could take far better than she did. It took a moment to get in a position where she had leverage, but then she reached forward, braced her opposite hand next to the wound, and yanked on the shaft with all her strength.

She could feel it fighting her. The tip was barbed; it tore flesh as she ripped it out. After it was free, she instinctively slapped a hand over the wound, trying to staunch the flow of blood as Christian hunched over, his breathing full of rattling and gargling sounds that gradually lessened, until within a minute he was able to look back up.

His wound wasn't gone, but it wasn't bleeding anymore.

While Christian leaned over, Alysia watched with a curious detachment as he snapped off the front of the bolt set in her knee, a move that should have caused agonizing pain, and then tugged the remainder of the shaft from her body before pushing himself to his feet.

Alysia looked at her wound long enough to convince herself that it wasn't gushing blood like it should have been and then accepted the hand Christian offered to help her stand.

The pain was gone, but the tendons or muscles or whatever were in the knee had been sliced up; there was no way her left leg would support her. She prayed Christian had some kind of a plan.

Thankfully, the recent storm had made an icy mess but had left little snow behind. They left no obvious tracks in the frozen ground as they limped together into the woods, Alysia leaning heavily on Christian to walk.

"If we cut through the woods this way, I think we'll get back to the gas station we passed," Christian said. "I can veil us so we won't be easily spotted."

"Isn't that the same technique that totally failed on Lynzi?" Alysia asked. She didn't want to be critical, but she did want to be realistic.

"She's one of my kind," Christian replied. "Harder to hide from. I—" He paused and leaned against the nearest tree for a minute before continuing. "I can keep us hidden from vamps and humans without using too much power."

He hadn't offered to heal her again. He could keep them hidden, but he didn't have any extra magic to burn.

The hike seemed to take forever. Alysia tried to ignore the way the numbness started to travel farther up her leg and the way her head started to spin. Pain was the body's way of saying, *We're broken. Stop everything and help me.* She didn't have time to stop, and she couldn't function with the pain, so she tried not to think how much more damage she was doing this way.

"I can't sense anyone except the human girl running the pumps," Christian said, "but the vamps do have that nasty habit of appearing unannounced. We should move fast."

"A stolen car will be reported in minutes," Alysia said as they reached the gas station, a one-pump, family-owned affair, "but we need transport. How are you at persuasion?"

"I think I can manage. You wait here, watch my back."

Stay out of the way, she heard, but since she was hobbled and just about useless at that moment, she decided not to take it personally.

She waited at the forest's edge while Christian approached the gas station. As he walked away, she began to feel her body again, starting with a vague ache in her knee, like a deep bruise or the soreness left behind after unusually heavy exercise. It wasn't intolerable, but it served as a warning.

It wasn't just for the sake of her own comfort that she hated watching him walk across the parking lot, though. She knew that few attackers would bother to take Christian on unless they were sure of a payout, which they would only get if they caught Alysia. Logically, that meant if they didn't see her, they shouldn't go after him. But logic didn't always dictate these things, and it didn't take into account the fact that Maya might still be holding a grudge against Christian and Alysia, who had wiped out almost a dozen of her brats six years earlier.

Christian leaned in to flirt with the cashier. Hopefully he could convince her to ignore the blood, hand over her keys, and then forget all about it. Meanwhile, Alysia watched for approaching vehicles. Christian would sense if anyone non-human approached, but that was little consolation when dealing with Bruja, and even a Triste did not have eyes in the back of his head.

The driver of the BMW convertible that pulled in at that moment was polite enough to have the top down, which meant Alysia recognized her instantly. She had been a member of Crimson back when Alysia had joined, and she still was, judging by Christian's wary expression when she called his name and he turned to look at her.

Alysia debated stepping forward, but waited. Christian looked cautious but not concerned, which meant he believed he could handle himself. Alysia wished she could make out what they were saying. The woman seemed to be asking questions, to which Christian gave terse responses.

They both turned toward the next vehicle that approached, a beat-up truck in which Alysia could see the driver one moment but not the next: vampire. The fact that he had disappeared was not a good sign. Alysia immediately turned, putting one of the larger trees to her back as she checked around her, which meant she wasn't looking when the truck exploded.

She threw herself flat and felt the double shock wave roll over her, first from the truck and then from the pumps. Her ears registered pressure more than sound, and her skin was aware of a slap of heat, though she was far enough away not to get the brunt of the blast.

Ash and debris were falling, but she started to vault back to her feet.

The pain hit her like whiplash. All the agony of a brutal injury that had been ignored and further abused for more than an hour crashed on her. No warning. No buildup, which would have helped her mind tolerate it.

She tried to draw the knife at her waist but wasn't fast enough to avoid a boot to the head and the inevitable blackness that followed.

She was walking down stairs. Everyone else in the house was asleep, but she wanted a drink of water. It was dark, but the path was familiar.

There was a noise in the living room.

Don't look, *she tried to tell her thirteen-year-old self, but of course a memory cannot listen. She went to look.*

She recognized him as the brother of one of her classmates. Why was he at her house at three in the morning? And why was he going through the box labeled "silver" that her parents had been fighting over for the last week?

Don't make a sound! Just turn away before he notices.

"Andy?" she asked.

He turned toward her with panic in his eyes. Even at that age, she could see the moment when he decided he had to shut her up.

She ran. He followed her, and that was when she went to the kitchen and grabbed a knife. He was more than a foot taller than she was, but she thought that once he realized she had a weapon, he would run away. He was supposed to run.

"Why didn't you run away?" she asked the memory. "Why did you—"

The memory shattered into reality as someone struck her. She struggled, fighting the impression that she was still grappling with Andy, and realized that her wrists were chained to the wall above her. She looked down and saw that someone had wrapped a bandage around her knee, and it was stained dark red. Seeing it made her queasy, and also made her realize she wasn't feeling as much pain as she should have been. Someone had drugged her, either chemically or magically.

"What—" She started to ask a question and discovered there was something wrong with her jaw. She was really not looking forward to what it was going to feel like when she started feeling pain again.

"I have one simple question for you," the man in front of her said.

She struggled to focus her vision and realized at last where she was, and who was with her. She was in one of the private rooms at the back of the Onyx Hall. Once upon a time, it had been a dressing room. There was even a shiny, framed painting left on the far wall, its silver and gold embroidery glinting in the light, as if the room were still used for something glamorous.

It wasn't. The once-polished floor was scuffed and scratched, not to mention bloodstained, and the walls hadn't been painted in decades. These days, Kral used this room as his own personal torture chamber. Just now, he was standing in front of Alysia with what she feared was her blood on his hands.

Alysia tried to draw a breath, but it only made her head spin. Her ribs shifted in a funny way, suggesting worse damage than she remembered suffering before she was knocked out.

"What was the question?" she managed to ask. A throbbing ache in her jaw warned her that the pain was not very far away.

"Where is she?"

Kral spoke slowly, clearly, in a way that betrayed it was

taking all his self-control for him not to snap her like kindling. Alysia had seen what it looked like when he didn't bother with that self-control, and she really did not want to bait him, but she didn't have the first idea what he wanted.

He was not going to like that excuse.

CHAPTER 14

"YOU'RE UPSET," JEHT observed as Sarik led the cubs back toward the front of the administration building.

The obvious reply, reminding him about the recent attack and the deadly fight that he had finished, would mean nothing to him. The less obvious answer, though, was much more complicated.

"Are you ever afraid?" she asked him as they entered the lobby and paused.

For a moment he looked offended; she saw the defensive answer form on his lips and the way he looked at his younger brother as if concerned about his reaction. Then he paused, taking in Sarik's expression. "Sometimes," he whispered. "When the blue men captured us, and then you came, I thought you would kill us."

Jeht and Quean had been picked up by human police after they had been thrown out of their own tribe, casualties of a coup that had overthrown the king, their father. It had taken time for SingleEarth to hear about them, to find someone who spoke their language, and then for Sarik to reach them.

Quean said in a tiny voice, "Sometimes I still think that."

Sarik resisted the urge to pick the smaller boy up and hug him tightly. He still saw her as his queen. Such an informal display would panic him.

"Sometimes I'm afraid, too," she admitted. "I'm afraid now, but there is nothing I can do about it. Every time I try to fix anything, people get hurt."

"Is the woman from earlier someone you hurt?" Jeht asked. "Is that why she is hunting you?"

"The woman who interrupted our meeting?" Sarik asked. Jeht wouldn't have understood anything the woman said, only that she had shouted a lot. "She's also afraid, I think," she answered. "Some people get angry when they're scared."

Jeht frowned. "She didn't smell angry or scared," he said. "She yelled like a tiger, like she was trying to frighten people, but her scent never changed except when she looked at you."

The words caught in Sarik's anxiety like a fishhook, tugging. Jeht was right—everyone in the room who spoke English had been focused on their own concerns and on the woman's words. They had all acknowledged that her behavior seemed "off," but none of them had consciously considered her body language.

"Mary," she asked as they entered the lobby, switching to English to speak to the secretary, "could I see the lobby tape from when our visitor came in?"

Mary pulled up the footage with a few clicks, then moved aside so Sarik and Jeht could see. Sarik watched and listened as the distressed woman who had come to look for Alysia paced and pleaded with the receptionist.

"Why isn't she here?" the woman demanded of Mary.

"She had to leave on business, I believe," Mary replied vaguely.

Sarik wondered if Mary had been fully informed yet about Alysia's situation, or if she was trying to make the situation seem less dire in an attempt to calm the woman.

"I have to see her."

"She isn't *here*." Mary was obviously losing her patience. "Please, let me show you to the conference room. The rest of the mediators are there. Maybe they can tell you more."

The woman nodded, her hand unconsciously going to a necklace barely visible at her throat, and then followed the receptionist out.

Sarik hit the Back button and watched the scene again, this time with no volume.

There was a moment when the woman looked up at the camera immediately upon entering, obviously noticing it and pondering its presence. In that moment, it was as if her gaze locked with Sarik's, and she seemed familiar in a way that made Sarik's heart pound.

She was dressed in an attractive but conservative style. Sarik remembered thinking how her clothing and hairstyle made the distinct shade of her hair less striking. Add colored contacts . . .

I know her.

They had met in another lifetime, when this woman had been an angry sixteen-year-old girl. She had been dressed in form-fitting black, with that burgundy hair cascading around her face, a perfect match to her eyes. Her gaze had fixed on the other angry young woman in the room, the tigress who glared at the newcomer with a warning to stay away.

Her name was Ravyn.

And she had come into SingleEarth and asked for Alysia, and then she had seen Sarik and established in a few angry sentences that Sarik was a tiger before she stormed out.

"Who is she?" Jeht asked.

Before Sarik could answer, Lynzi emerged with her phone at her ear, saying, "We'll be there within the hour."

Lynzi saw Sarik and waved her over as she continued toward the parking lot.

"That was one of the local hospitals," she explained. "They called us to say they had someone in who was healing unusually and might be more our kind of patient. I can't tell for sure from the description, but I think it's Christian. The doctor said there was a young woman with him, apparently human, also severely hurt and unconscious. Pandora probably already knows if her student is in danger, but I'm not sure she'll bother to help Alysia, so I'm going. Jason is scheduling a meeting with Maya." Her phone rang. She glanced down and said, "That's Diana. I called her in case I need help at the hospital. Hello?" she said, answering the call. "Wait, is—"

Lynzi didn't bother to wait to hear what else Sarik might say. Humans were so fragile; minutes, even seconds, could matter if Alysia was severely injured.

As for Christian, it was hard to know. As Sarik understood it, Triste witches could heal almost anything, but healing required concentration and concentration required consciousness. If Christian was unconscious, he could very well die if his injuries were severe and no one was close enough to help.

He could die.

She wasn't at all sure how she felt about that. Her body and mind seemed numb and full of static.

"My lady?" Jeht inquired.

She told him, because she needed to tell someone. "Someone I was once close to might be seriously hurt."

Christian Denmark was one of the most dangerous people she had ever met, in general and to her in particular. She had been so careful to keep herself in silhouette so he could not get a good look at her at the Onyx Hall and to keep him from ever seeing her face after that.

Why did she now want to run to the hospital to make sure he was okay?

Because it was too late for it to matter.

"The woman who was attacked earlier?" Jeht asked.

"She's hurt, too," Sarik said. "And it's my fault. I . . ." How to put it into terms that the young Mistari would understand? "I chose to leave my tribe six years ago. I did not tell my father-king or the mate he had chosen for me that I was leaving or where I was going. I ran away and I hid, because I knew he would look for me. Jason ran from his . . . his queen . . . and we came here together. The woman you asked about will tell my father where I am."

Just saying the words made her mouth dry. Scenes from her childhood—and of that final, horrible day—flashed through her mind.

"You fear he will bring you back, *ra'nasgel*?" Jeht asked.

The term literally meant "obedient child," and implied being under another's power—specifically, in this case, the tribe's leader.

She nodded, which caused Jeht's confused frown to deepen.

"Can you fight him?" he asked.

She shook her head. "He is very strong, and has many allies."

Lynzi and Alysia had both said it: SingleEarth could not afford a direct conflict with the Bruja guilds. SingleEarth probably had more political power, and possibly more money, but Kral would not hesitate to kill to get his daughter back. Sarik wouldn't let herself be responsible for the deaths that would inevitably occur if SingleEarth tried to stand up to Onyx.

If she tried to stay at SingleEarth, he would come for her. He might hesitate to target someone like Diana, but he would certainly kill Jason—because he would want to punish her and because Jason had belonged to Maya. For similar reasons, Sarik couldn't run. Kral had tracked her this far. Disappearing again would put everyone she had formed a connection with during the last six years in danger.

She didn't have a choice.

"We're leaving," she told the boys.

They didn't question her; even Quean probably understood.

She had left Onyx of her own free will six years ago, and she had survived her self-imposed exile. If she returned without being forced and declared herself independent, then by Mistari law she had to be respected as a queen. In Kral's territory, she would still be under his command to an extent, but she could claim sovereignty over Jeht and Quean and could keep Kral from them long enough to get them back to the main tribes. If she needed to go back for now in order to keep SingleEarth safe, she would at least accomplish something by getting the cubs home.

Anger rose, at last, burning bright. It was the same anger that had sustained her growing up in Onyx. It was the fury that had allowed her to face the blood and the violence, and had erased any sign of fear from her face and her conscious mind. She had put that anger away when she had joined SingleEarth, but now she needed it.

The anger threatened to recede only once, when she went to pack a few belongings and to leave a message for Jason.

It wasn't supposed to work out this way.

When she'd found the weapons after breaking into Alysia's room, she had been certain that no Bruja member of such high rank could possibly be in SingleEarth without an ulterior motive. Alysia had to be there for a job, or because she was being hunted by someone even more dangerous than herself. Sarik had panicked, certain that *she* was the one Alysia was hunting. The memo looking for someone who spoke ha'Mistari had gone up just before Alysia had suddenly expressed an interest in a mediator's position. Alysia knew, or suspected, and even if she hadn't known before applying for the mediator job, she could make the connection too easily once she saw Sarik. And a visit from a third-ranked member of any of the Bruja guilds normally ended with someone dead.

Diana was already gone. If Lynzi had known about Sarik's suspicions, she would have confronted Alysia and tipped her off but then given her a chance to explain herself, because SingleEarth was all about second chances.

So Sarik had grabbed the crossbow and bolts and followed Alysia into the storm, planning to shoot one bolt in the human's back and then plant the others in her room. After the weapons were discovered, her death would have been blamed on some kind of guild conflict.

But Sarik hadn't been able to go through with the kill. Head swirling with nightmares and panic, she had pointed the crossbow at Alysia but had been unable to pull the trigger. When the three shapes had emerged from the administration building, it had for a few seconds seemed so clear: no one needed to die. After the attack, Sarik could confide to Lynzi that she had seen a weapon in Alysia's room, and the human would be forced out of SingleEarth in a heartbeat.

It had only taken a few seconds to do the stupidest thing she had ever done in her life.

Everything had gone wrong, karma coming back to bite her. Jason had walked outside, and Alysia hadn't done anything Sarik had expected. An undercover Bruja mercenary wouldn't have run forward and risked herself to take care of other SingleEarth members. She wouldn't have bled to help Jason.

Now Alysia was in the hospital, and it was all Sarik's fault.

They would hate her if they knew.

She deserved it.

CHAPTER 15

THERE WAS NO getting around it—Alysia had to ask.

"Where is *who*?"

Kral just kind of nudged her, and that was enough to send flares of pain to her brain from her leg and her ribs. She gasped, trying not to pass out again . . . or wait, passing out might be good at the moment . . . but no, she stayed conscious. And when the pain pushed the drugs aside for a second, she managed to figure out what he was asking.

When Alysia had first joined Onyx, Kral had wanted to know the same thing: the whereabouts of his daughter, Sahara. She had disappeared right before Alysia had first come to Onyx.

"I told you before," she choked out, "I've never met her."

The fact that he might kill her had occurred to her intellectually but hadn't really hit her yet. He might kill her. He might let the drugs wear off and just allow her to die from shock or infection. He might torture her to death.

She was pretty sure that would bother her eventually.

"She disappeared within twenty-four hours of your appearance on Onyx's doorstep," Kral declared. "Six years later, I hear that you've dropped by Onyx, and my daughter calls me within the next twenty-four hours. It is too wild a coincidence for the two to be unrelated."

"I can see why it seems that way," Alysia said.

Upon saying it, she realized how incredibly stupid she had been.

No, not stupid—uninformed.

Alysia had never known Sahara. She had seen pictures of the wild, leather-garbed huntress who was princess of the Onyx guild and who, as one novice had described it, had displayed Christian a bit like a fur stole, but she had never seen the tigress in person, never tried to picture what she might look like without the metal and the screw-the-world attitude.

Think it through. Don't sic Kral on SingleEarth, not on such a crazy theory. Clear-minded, she probably wouldn't begin to believe that the sweet little mediator could be the same tigress who had left four neat scars in a row across Christian's chest.

That argument had been the final straw. He had walked out, taken the job against Maya despite Kral's forbidding it, and hooked up with Alysia.

Kral slapped her, relatively softly but hard enough to get her attention.

"What did you give me?" Alysia asked. "I can't think. Can't answer your questions if I can't think."

"It's an easy question. You know the answer."

Whether she did or not, she didn't want to tell him jack until she was able to think through the consequences.

Which was why he had drugged her.

Goddamn.

The impact made her ache enough that it took her a moment to realize she hadn't been the one hit. Something very large and solid had struck the door from the outside. The door opened and an unconscious guard fell into Kral.

Behind the guard was a slender woman with hair and eyes the color of spilled blood. Even at this distance, Alysia recognized her, though her hair was now shorn very short in a style that did not look entirely intentional. In fact, it was a little singed, as was the skin on her left hand.

Flatly, she informed Kral, "Your merc blew up my new car."

"Ravyn, can't you see I'm *busy*?"

Ravyn glanced at Alysia, then back at Kral. "Yeah, real busy. And you owe me a Beamer. Also, Pandora is pissed that you sent her student to the hospital, and I had a chat with your daughter this morning. But you're *busy*, so I'll be on my way."

She turned around and dodged when Kral reached for her. The knife appeared in her hand like magic as she spat, "Put a hand on me and I will put a *hole* in you, tiger. Is that clear? I just came to tell you I expect you to replace that car, and I want you to keep your family feud in your own guild. If I hear you're soliciting underranked Crimson members again—for a hit on *SingleEarth*, of all the pathetic things—you and I are going to have words and weapons."

"Um, help?" Alysia managed to ask when it became clear that Ravyn was about to leave and Kral was going to let her walk out.

"Onyx business is not my deal," Ravyn replied.

Mercenaries, Alysia thought.

Kral's response was a little less resigned. He turned around with a growl and smacked Alysia hard enough that the world turned pink, then gray, then white, and then was gone completely.

Alysia tried to run.

Andy followed her. She went to the kitchen and grabbed a knife. He was more than a foot taller than she was, but she thought that once he realized she had a weapon, he would run away. He probably didn't want to fight.

When he reached for her, she ran again, toward the stairs, shouting for her parents, her mother in the bedroom and her father on an air mattress in the study. She cut her hand when Andy grabbed her ankle. She stumbled, and they tussled on the stairs.

Alysia's father appeared at the top landing, but not in time to keep them both from falling and rolling down the wooden steps, knife between them. She was vaguely aware of the knife blade sliding into flesh, an instant before they reached the bottom and she came to a sudden stop as the back of her skull slammed into flagstone tile.

She woke with a doctor and a police officer at her side. She did not need to ask what had happened to Andy, because in that final second, she had felt the knife and the blood and seen the look in his eyes. She looked at the cop and burst into tears. She was a murderer. They would arrest her.

Alysia woke with a start and then moaned as her sudden movement pulled on her chains.

The worst part had been that she had known him.

No, the worst part had been waking up in a hospital and being assured that it was perfectly fine that she had killed a classmate. He had broken into their house, probably looking for something to sell for drug money, and apparently that made it all right that she had murdered him. Everything she did after that, she was assured by her mother's therapist, was "perfectly normal" and all right because of her parents' pending divorce and the little issue of a murder no one seemed to care about.

Staying out late. Getting in trouble. Stealing a pair of sneakers. Stealing a Lexus. Hacking into the school network. Hacking into the *police* network. Breaking into a swanky house in a suburban neighborhood only to find herself in the middle of a guild of ruthless assassins. The leader of Frost, a terrifying woman named Sarta, had given her an opportunity to join her guild or go to jail for a long time. Alysia would have joined even without the threat. Her mother's therapist probably would have told her that she used contracts from Frost to fill the void left behind by two parents who meant well but were too focused on their own fears and needs to question their daughter further when she assured them she was fine.

You're not fine now, she reminded herself, struggling to focus and pull her thoughts back to the present. Whatever drugs

Kral had given her were obviously still in her system, making her mind wander in all sorts of inconvenient ways, but they were starting to wear off. The evidence of that was the screaming pain running up and down her body like an electric current.

If Kral believed what Ravyn had said about having a "chat" with his daughter, he had probably gone after her for more information. Alysia was alone for the moment, but she didn't know how long that would last.

Her hands were mostly numb from being above her head for so long. She couldn't clench her teeth against the pain of trying to lift her head to examine the shackles because her jaw refused to cooperate, so she just breathed shallowly and tried not to wonder how many ribs were broken.

Some people liked metal shackles. They were cruel and cold, and most people feared them. On the plus side, they tended not to be adjustable. Kral no doubt had a variety of sizes—because if you're prone to chaining people in your greenroom, you would have to, right?—but in the end, the iron rings rarely fit well.

Alysia twisted her right hand, letting the muscles go slack as she forced her thumb out of joint. Someday she wanted to do a survey on how many Bruja members were double-jointed, especially in their hands; it seemed like a great evolutionary advantage to Alysia, who had wriggled out of more restraints than most people in safer professions ever had to worry about.

Everything went gray as she hit the ground and her legs collapsed under her. It took at least a century, maybe an eon, for the pain to recede. She couldn't seem to get enough air, and her heart was pounding.

She shouldn't stand up. If she did, she would faint, and she couldn't afford to faint. She used her hands to get closer to the door and reached up to test the knob. Raising her arm so far above her head brought the black patches back to her vision, but it was worth it when she found the door unlocked.

As hell-bent as Kral was on tracking down Sahara, he probably wouldn't stop to worry that a mere human might have the fortitude to escape. He hadn't bothered to lock the door. He probably hadn't taken the time to replace the guard Ravyn had incapacitated, either.

Alysia opened the door a crack. The Onyx Hall was kept dark, which would work in her favor, but she still needed to get outside so she could get to a car and a phone.

Unfortunately, she needed to stand first, which she did very carefully and incrementally with the help of a red oak bo staff someone had been kind enough to leave lying about. She debated grabbing some of the other weapons that had been left along the back wall, but if she ended up trying to use them, she would only fall over anyway.

Besides, she was a member of Frost. The staff was deadly enough, if she could manage to lift it.

She had to pause to catch her breath once she was outside, but then she circled the building until she found a beat-up old Jeep that looked like it had gone off-roading and possibly rolled down a mountain at least once. She wasn't the first to check out its electrical guts, either; the panel was already missing.

Getting in the seat left her panting and sweating, but she managed. Once she was a little farther away, she would find a phone and call a hospital . . . and possibly SingleEarth, since they would help with her injuries even if they believed that she was a coldhearted killer.

Shock and adrenaline kept Alysia going as she eased out of the parking lot, grateful that the Jeep had an automatic transmission. Her body did not have any energy to support fear or anger, but she was vaguely aware that if this was Sarik's fault, the tiger would have to pay in some slow and painful manner.

A car horn blared at her and she jumped. She had zoned out and drifted into the opposite lane. She wasn't going to get far this way.

Just get me to civilization. Even an exploding gas station would be a relief.

CHAPTER 16

LYNZI HAD NO idea what she was asking of him.

Jason knew that was his fault. He had told Lynzi that he had worked for Maya, but he had never explained what that meant. Maya didn't have *employees*, she had slaves.

According to vampiric law, Jason belonged to her, but Maya didn't value her "possessions" more highly than cash. She wouldn't refuse to negotiate with SingleEarth. It was only habit that made it seem to him that she would try to snatch him back, when rationally he knew that she would consider giving up one pawn a small price to pay for SingleEarth's favor. Maya was practical.

He had to keep telling himself that as he picked up his phone. He didn't know a direct number for her these days, but he was confident that he could find her. After all, what use was a mercenary if no one could reach her to hire her?

Alysia would have been the natural choice for this job. She had a history in Bruja; she knew how to speak the language of payout that piqued a mercenary's interest. But she was in the hospital now, collateral damage of the current conflict.

He dialed, knowing there was no chance that Maya herself would pick up. He spoke to "florists" and "jewelers" and "caterers," always leaving the same message: *Tell Maya to call Jason at SingleEarth Haven Number Four.*

Some of the numbers probably were those of legitimate businesses that had never heard of Maya. It had been six years, after all. But he was sure that some of the contact places he knew were still taking messages. She would hear.

It has been six years, he thought, but the number wasn't much of a comfort. He had been thirteen when she had picked him up. Seventeen when she had changed him. He wasn't sure how many years had passed after that before he met Sarik. Not many, he thought, but time spent with Maya was a haze of trying never to think. Trying to survive the day.

He left messages, grateful that he did not have to hear her voice just yet, and then returned to the residential building. He needed to rest. No, he needed Sarik. He needed her to remind him that he wasn't the creature Maya had tried to make him.

When he reached their room, though, Sarik wasn't there. Instead, he found a note scrawled in her handwriting on a piece of SingleEarth stationery. The pen still lay nearby.

Jason,

I've lied to you. I've hurt you. I'm doing what I can now to make amends. I need to leave. Please don't look for me. I love you.

–Sarik

He stared at the note. Picked it up. Read it again. Saw in the black ink a telltale wavering that said her hand had been shaking while she'd written these words.

The only thing missing from the room, beyond Sarik herself, was the bag in which she stored her identification, cash, and credit cards—items she never needed at the Haven but that she kept handy for when she needed to go out into the world.

Where are you, Sarik?

He sent himself to the cubs' enclosure, where his sudden appearance made Mark jump nearly out of his skin and exclaim, "Don't do that!"

"Sorry. Do you know where Sarik is?"

He could already tell that the cubs were gone. Even if they had been sleeping inside, he would have been able to hear their heartbeats.

"She said she was taking the boys on a field trip," Mark answered. "It seemed like a good idea to me."

It would have been, if she'd been planning to come back.

If she had taken the cubs with her, she could only be going

one place: back to her father, the abusive bastard who had so completely terrified and dominated her for sixteen years that even now, the merest mention of him made her freeze like a squirrel facing an oncoming car.

Please don't look for me, her note had said.

I'm sorry, love, but that's one request I am never going to grant.

How many Mistari tribes were there in the United States? It couldn't be that hard to track down the one she—

Jason's cell phone rang, and this time it was his turn to feel like a small animal staring into the bright glare of headlights.

He stepped away from Mark before he answered the phone.

"Hello?"

"It is you!" The voice on the other side was light, cheerful even. One of the first thoughts he had ever had about Maya, when she had found him homeless on the streets, was that she had a lovely voice. "When my Paulo told me I had a message from Jason, I was sure it had to be someone else. It's such a common name. But now that I'm sure—"

He let out a yelp as she appeared in front of him, ending the call as she met his gaze with her own black one.

"I am so looking forward to hearing your explanation. How're you doing, darling?"

Words fled.

As usual, Maya was dressed to the nines, which today meant designer jeans, a scarlet kimono-style blouse, three throwing daggers on her left wrist, and a katana in an elaborate sheath at her left hip. Though she originally hailed from Cape Verde, sometime in the last half decade she had apparently developed a taste for Japanese fashion, which meant her thick brown hair was pinned up on top of her head in a style Jason associated with high school girls fascinated with anime.

On the other hand, the adorable pink rhinestone hairstick he could see was probably sharpened to a deadly point treated with poison.

Jason noticed three hunters creeping closer and held up a hand, indicating that they should pause. He said to Maya, "I work here now. I called you for a business meeting that you might find profitable. Are you going to be professional, or are you just here to play?"

She grinned. "You know I could take out your hunters before they could blink an eye, don't you?"

"I don't know that," he replied, "and neither do you. Do you want to work or not?"

He was certain she wouldn't risk a fight unless she was pushed to it—she was a businesswoman, after all—but that didn't mean she wouldn't try to push his buttons. He didn't know how long he could keep up this confident façade if she decided to test him.

Instead, she sighed. "I suppose I can see what you have to offer before I decide what I want. Let's go somewhere comfortable and you can get me some tea. Then we'll talk about how you killed Liam and now want to make amends."

The words took him aback just long enough that she was able to lead the way toward the administration building. As he hurried after her, one of the hunters increased his pace to catch up.

"Is there a problem?" the hunter asked.

"Not yet," Jason answered, "but if you're willing to stay close, that would be good."

Did Maya know she wouldn't be able to simply disappear from inside any of these buildings? She might not. He wasn't sure what kind of advantage that might give him, but it was good to know anyway.

"Mary, can you get us some green tea?" he asked as they passed the secretary's desk. "We'll be in conference room one."

Maya glanced back just long enough to see which door he gestured to and to say "Good boy" in response to his choice of beverage.

Given her current fashion choices, green tea hadn't been a deductive stretch. The only other possibility had been bubble tea, but he was pretty sure Mary didn't keep that on hand.

Maya sat herself at the head of the conference table, leaned back to put her feet up, and then said, "So, Jason. What happened to Liam?"

"He tried to either kill or abduct a SingleEarth mediator," Jason answered.

"Correction. He tried to abduct a third-ranked member of Frost, Onyx, *and* Crimson," she replied as she fiddled absently with one of six buckles on her knee-high boot. "Said member is guilty of just about every crime written by human *or* witch authorities, and therefore not eligible for sanctuary in SingleEarth."

"It isn't about what she used to be."

"No, it's about who she *is*," Maya retorted. "She's a killer and a thief. Not that I'm judging, but SingleEarth does. And you're asking all the wrong questions."

"Then what should I be asking?"

She raised one brow and waited.

"You were hired to go after Alysia," he said.

Maya nodded. "It was a public posting." *Public* meant she had no reason to withhold the information, since it had no value.

"Who hired you?"

"That part isn't public."

He made a mental note and moved on.

"Do you know anything about the job that resulted in me and two others being shot here recently?"

"You were shot? Poor baby," she replied. "I had no idea. But if I were you, I would ask one of the two highly ranked members of Onyx who have been here in the last week. Maybe the one whose sister you murdered."

She was volunteering information, which meant she was trying to hurt him, but he couldn't immediately guess what she was implying. He was sure he had murdered *somebody's* sister during his time with Maya, but how was he supposed to know that anyone here at Haven #4 was a survivor of one of those kills?

Alysia could be. If she had recognized him as the monster who had killed someone in her family, she might have been swift to take revenge, even if she *had* otherwise reformed. That would explain the timing of the attack but not why someone had hired Maya to capture Alysia.

"Wait for it," Maya said, leaning forward with a slight smile, at the same moment that all the puzzle pieces came together in his head.

"Sarik," he said.

Sarik, who was so terrified of her father, who had made him into some kind of godlike figure in her mind, one even SingleEarth couldn't stand up to. Who had blanched when Jason had mentioned Kral. He had thought the reaction was because she was afraid the leader of Onyx would mention her to her father, but . . .

"No," he said, standing up.

"Darling," Maya said sweetly, "has your lover been less than honest with you?"

Sarik had told him that she had ended up in Maya's care because she had stupidly knocked on the door looking for help because she had run away from home and become lost. She hadn't been lost. She had been looking for Cori, the girl Maya had been hired to kidnap.

Maya stood up and came to his side. She patted his shoulder and leaned against his side to say, "Love hurts, darling. And I don't think you have any deal worth offering me, so I'm going to head out. I'll look you up next time I need something."

She walked away, just in time for Mary to arrive with her tea. Mary looked bewildered that the meeting was already over. Jason followed Maya, only to make sure the hunters would let her go. No one here wanted a fight.

As soon as Maya had disappeared, Jason collapsed in one of the chairs in the reception room. He didn't know what to do next. Where to go next.

"Jason?" Mary asked. "Is everything all right?"

He shook his head.

When Lynzi got home, he would tell her.

Tell her *what,* exactly?

He could tell her what she wanted to know, he decided: that SingleEarth wasn't at risk for further attacks. After all, Alysia and Sarik—

Sahara. He knew her name as well as he knew Christian's and Kral's.

Alysia and Sahara were gone.

Sarik was gone.

CHAPTER 17

CHRISTIAN DRIFTED IN and out of consciousness for a while. Each time he came close to the surface, he tried to grab on to reality enough to focus, but it was hard.

Once, he heard someone say to someone else near him, "The woman they found was the cashier working at the station. She says she doesn't remember seeing Alysia."

Christian tried to ask a question on that topic, but the effort caused the world to slip away again.

The next time he woke, he could feel someone funneling power into him. It wasn't Pandora, but it had to be another of his own kind.

She must have sensed his mental nearness, because she said, "If you're awake enough to help me out, give me a sign."

He tried, but he couldn't focus.

Again he woke, and finally he was able to get a sense of his body. He was hurt, badly, but Lynzi had probably saved his life. He managed to ask mentally, *Where's Pandora?*

She came, Lynzi replied, the same way. *She said this was your "own stupid fault" and that as long as you already have a Single-Earth nursemaid, she doesn't need to waste her time.*

That sounded like her.

It also finally gave Christian the motivation he needed to focus his power, so the next time his body demanded rest, his mind went into a trance instead of to sleep. Externally, the state looked much the same, but internally, he was able to start stitching himself back together. Ruptured blood vessels closed and strengthened. Fractured bones and crushed organs regained their proper shapes and places.

All the while, Lynzi continued to slowly drip power into him so he could heal the damage, which was worse than his body had ever before sustained. He was vaguely aware when the flavor of the power changed, which meant Lynzi had probably had one of her SingleEarth underlings come in to feed her.

The power sustaining him spiked, like a shock of static electricity. *Those "underlings" are responsible for saving your life,* Lynzi remarked, reading his thoughts. *You might want to consider that.*

Right. Have they found Alysia?

Not yet, Lynzi answered. *Once you're recovered enough to actually talk, I expect you to explain everything.*

Sure.

She had to know he was lying, but she let it slide.

An intrusion of fear and anger pushed him out of his trance. Pure wrath had just walked through the door.

His eyes flickered open, but it took several seconds for them to focus. And then . . .

He knew that mouth, those eyes, those cheekbones. The way she would pout and expect the world on a platter, and— *Damn her.* Did she have any idea—

Pandora would not approve, but he didn't care. He let the fury well through him as he reached for the tiger, a hand locking around her throat and power digging into her guts so he could drag the energy from her.

Her body spasmed, but he knew that her throat would be too tight for her to scream.

He could ignore Lynzi's shout, but he couldn't ignore Sahara's reaction, which was to change shape from a beautiful woman to a form of fur and muscle—a form that included sharp teeth and claws that ripped into Christian's shoulder and chest, forcing him to let her go.

The instant he released her, she let herself fall back into human form.

They both ignored Lynzi frantically shouting their names— well, not *her* name, not really.

Sahara coughed once and rubbed her throat before saying, "Just like old times."

One hand over the bleeding claw marks in his shoulder, Christian waved Lynzi back and answered, "Not *just* like." He had pulled enough power out of Sahara before she forced him to stop that he was able to keep the new wounds from bleeding, but he couldn't do more. Still, it was enough to make his point. He wasn't the same human kid she had known six years earlier.

"Are you all right?" Sahara asked, at the same moment that he demanded, "Where's Alysia?"

Lynzi tried to intercede, saying, "Christian, I told you—"

Sahara cut her off, asking, "She's not here?"

She wasn't feigning ignorance. Her skin paled and her breath hitched as the only other possibility occurred to her. If Alysia wasn't in the hospital, then she had to be with the person who had offered the money to abduct her. Sahara's presence here made it damn clear who that was.

"Lynzi, Christian and I have to go," she said.

"I think we need to *talk*," Lynzi replied. "And Christian shouldn't—"

"I'll be fine," Christian interrupted. "Sahara, come on."

"Absolutely not," Lynzi objected, grabbing his arm.

Christian could feel the crackle of her power like static electricity. He knew that given his current weakened state, she could take him down in an instant.

"It's okay, Lynzi," Sahara said, reassuring the witch with a soft tone and a forced smile. "Christian and I have . . . a history. His reaction is understandable. And he's right that I need to go with him. I can't explain now, but I will call as soon as I can."

Lynzi stared at Sahara, hearing every half-truth in her words, Christian was certain—especially the bit about *I will call as soon as I can*. Sahara had no intention of calling.

"If it's your choice to leave, Sarik, then I won't hold you here."

She released Christian's arm reluctantly, not entirely withdrawing her power until the last moment. He stood, and Sahara came to his side. He looped an arm over her shoulders, and she wrapped one around his waist, as if six years hadn't passed since the last time they had leaned against each other, concealing exhaustion and weakness under a veneer of companionship.

Each step hurt, but Christian trusted that he could keep his body under control long enough to find out whether Alysia was safe.

"Does Kral have Alysia?" he asked.

"I don't know," Sahara answered, "but if she isn't here, then I'm afraid it's likely."

"What are you going to do?" His instinct was to haul Sahara back to her father, trussed like a Thanksgiving turkey, but in his current state, he had to hope she didn't plan to fight him.

"I have to face my father," she said in a small voice.

If that was her plan, then she would come with him willingly.

"I need to make a call," he said as they reached the reception room, where a very stern, disapproving secretary saw him and instantly started forward with a frown that made him realize he was wearing a hospital gown. Given the damage his body had sustained, he suspected his clothes were not in any shape for him to put back on.

"That's fine," Sahara answered. "I need to—"

Ignoring Sahara for the moment, Christian forestalled the secretary's protest by catching her hand and shoving the thought into her head: *There's no problem here.* It was about as subtle as he could be right now.

"I'll be back in a minute," Sahara said while Christian dealt with the now utterly bewildered secretary.

He didn't like letting her walk away, but she wasn't going toward an exit. He kept an eye on the hall she would need to pass through if she wanted to flee. Meanwhile, the secretary graciously brought him behind the desk and handed him her cell phone, since, like his clothes, his own phone was probably useless.

He dialed and a surly female voice answered, "Yeah?"

"You owe me one hell of a favor," he informed the leader of Crimson. He had seen the explosion coming an instant before she had, giving him just enough time to shove the burgundy-haired human out of the way and take the brunt of the blast himself.

"Christian," Ravyn replied flatly. "You're alive."

"Don't sound so disappointed."

"I hate owing people favors," she answered, "but I'm good for this one. Which girl do you want me to retrieve, and in how many pieces do you want the tiger?"

Speaking of tigers, Sahara had just returned to the lobby and was walking toward him.

"I've . . ."

Christian trailed off, because Sahara wasn't alone. *What the hell?* He stared at the two children with her. How old were they? Aside from a few twisted individuals like Kral, few members of Bruja exposed their children to their work, if they

had children at all. As a result, Christian had little experience
judging the ages of little people.

"Frost?" Ravyn asked. "You still there?"

"Get Alysia," he said. "I have the tigers. Tiger."

He had to brace himself on the edge of the counter as he
stood. He dropped the phone and didn't bother to pick it up.
He really hoped Sahara wasn't planning to put up a fight, because he wasn't entirely sure he could win against even the
toddler-sized kid with her. Kids with Mistari features, obvious Mistari blood.

Sahara said something softly to the older kid and then
walked back to Christian's side. "Christian, this is Jeht and
Quean," she said, utterly failing to provide the information he
wanted. "I need to drop them off somewhere safe first, but you
and I have to get to Onyx as soon as possible. If Kral has—"

"Are they yours?" Christian asked, because obviously Sahara wasn't concerned with explaining why she had two children following her.

"Yes," she snapped. "Are you listening? If Alysia isn't
here, then she's—" She broke off, her eyes widening. "Yes,
they're *with* me, and they're my responsibility and nominally
part of my tribe at the moment," she clarified, "but no, they're
not *mine*. Don't you think you would have known if I had a kid
when I was *thirteen*?"

The older one was nine, then. Christian bit back his response, which would have been that he'd had no idea how
old the kid was and had been terrified that he could be *six*.
There were certainly stranger reasons why a sixteen-year-old
girl might run away from home.

Of course, he knew exactly why Sahara had run. He and Alysia had found Cori's body in that cellar. Christian and Sahara had done what they could to protect her, but that sweet human girl had been nothing but cannon fodder from the moment Kral had made his disinterest clear.

"I know you want to get to Alysia—I do, too—but I don't want to bring the cubs to Onyx," Sarik said. "Doing so will only put them in my father's power. Do you know a place—"

"They can stay at my house for now," Christian said. "It's on the way, and given our past relationship, it meets the letter of Mistari law in terms of having them in your territory."

Normally Christian wouldn't have been so swift to let anyone into his space, but he wanted to get to Alysia, he didn't have the energy to argue with Sahara, and he absolutely agreed that the boys shouldn't be brought within ten miles of Kral. As long as they remained in Sahara's territory, she could legally claim them as her own. The six years that had passed did not negate the fact that, once upon a time, Kral had set Christian up as Sahara's mate. That made his territory hers by Mistari law—law he would call upon only insofar as it was convenient. Keeping the boys safe was one thing, but if *Sahara* intended to move in, they were going to need to renegotiate.

At least going by his house would give him a chance to get some real clothes. The hospital gown was a little drafty for a dramatic confrontation with an ancient tiger.

A wave of dizziness hit him as they entered the elevator. Sahara caught his arm, and they both stumbled.

"Are you okay?" she asked.

"He's hurt?" the older kid asked.

It had been years since Christian had heard or spoken ha'Mistari, but as long as Jeht stuck to simple, two-word phrases using familiar words, he could follow.

Sahara, however, replied in rapid speech that made no sense to him at all. She then switched back to English to ask Christian, "Well, are you?"

"I'll be better when we find Alysia," he answered.

He certainly wasn't up to a fight with the old tiger, but if Kral had taken Alysia in order to track down his daughter, then hopefully showing up with Sahara would make him realize that continuing to hold his prisoner was unnecessary.

You're pushing yourself to the point of stupid.

He could practically hear Pandora's voice in his head. Most of the last year had been devoted to learning how far his body and mind could be pushed. Right now, he was burning too many resources just to keep himself functioning. He needed to feed, heal, and truly *rest*.

Soon, he promised himself. *Soon*.

CHAPTER 18

IT WAS EARLY evening when they reached the Onyx Hall, so the place was busy. Six years earlier, Sahara would have appreciated that; she'd always loved making an entrance. Sarik was less pleased with the way heads swiveled toward them when she and Christian stepped through the door.

Christian was leaning on her shoulder in a way that probably looked possessive, or at least friendly. Others couldn't tell how much of his weight she was supporting. They also didn't know there was a tacit threat in his touch. If she tried to wriggle away before they reached her father, she was sure she would be treated to another taste of the Triste's power.

Even the novices who had never seen Sahara kuloka Kral seemed to recognize the sudden buzz among the older members. The whispers made the spot along her spine between her shoulder blades crawl, expecting a knife. How many wounds, bruises, and broken bones had she received in this place—or given, for that matter? Kral had insisted that only by being the strongest could she make others fear her enough to follow her, obey her, never cross her, either to her face or behind her back. In the end, it hadn't been enough. Cori had been the example that Sahara's enemies had made for her, their way of showing her that she wasn't strong enough to protect anything, even her own sister.

"Where's Kral?" Christian asked the nearest archer, a younger member Sahara didn't recognize.

"Somewhere around here," the archer answered. He swept his gaze up and down Sarik's form, his expression openly skeptical and insolent. It was not a look she ever would have tolerated in the old days, but she had been back barely seconds, and she was tired. Of Christian, he asked, "Who's the—"

Christian didn't let him finish. Without even needing to remove his arm from Sarik's waist, Christian put the archer on the floor with one graceful, practiced move.

I've been gone too long, she thought. It was going to take time for her to relearn all the habits that had protected her for so many years. Onyx had humans and non-tiger shapeshifters and Tristes, but Kral ran it like a Mistari clan. It was not a place where one could afford to be tired.

Christian had pulled her from the proverbial frying pan, but it was still sizzling around here.

Sarik did not address the archer on the ground. Threats were generally made by people who were bluffing. "Let's find my father," she said, confirming the whispered speculation that she could hear all around her.

"He's in his office," another man chimed in. Sarik looked at him, wondering if she should know who he was. He was wearing a baggy sweatshirt that only mostly concealed the results of a recent beating. "I'm Kevin," he said.

"One of Kral's flunkies," Christian told her. "He had fewer bruises last time I saw him, though. Let's go."

Kevin led them through the crowd, which parted before them, and then knocked on Kral's office door.

Kral's response was barely audible, a growled, "What?"

The sound made the hair on the back of Sarik's neck stand up. Kevin flinched as well before he said, "Sir. I have your daughter here."

Silence. Then, after too many rapid hummingbird heartbeats, "Send her in."

Kevin opened the door and quickly backed away. Christian released Sarik and leaned against the doorjamb. She wasn't sure if Christian couldn't stand on his own or if he was blocking her exit in case she panicked and tried to run. She took a few steps into the room. The dim light from the single desk lamp made the office into a cave.

This room had always frightened her. Shapeshifters could heal more than humans could, and Bruja members weren't the type to call the police or social services, so her father had never needed to use restraint when he disciplined her. This room had meant countless beatings when she was a child.

"*Divai, ohne,*" she said. Her voice was soft, but at least it didn't break. "I've come home."

"Indeed," Kral said flatly.

The single word raked down her spine like claws. *You're not sixteen anymore,* she told herself. *You survived on your own. You were a mediator at SingleEarth. You cannot let him control you.*

But she couldn't seem to find her voice.

Kral looked at Christian. "Are you the one responsible for bringing her home?"

Sarik tensed and was about to protest that she had chosen to return on her own, but Christian asked his own question instead.

"Where is Alysia?"

Kral paused a moment, seeming contemplative. "If you do not know, then I'm sure I don't."

"You tried to frame her for the attack on SingleEarth, and then put a number up on her," Christian said.

"Oh, really?" Kral glanced at Sarik. He knew, or guessed, that at least part of the story Christian told had been her fault, but he had no reason to share that information. He also apparently had no interest in continuing the conversation. "Daughter, there is a rumor going around that you are starting your own tribe. You don't seriously expect to challenge me, do you?"

"No," she snapped instinctively. "I mean, yes, but—" *Get a hold of yourself!* She took a deep breath and drew on the calm, controlled persona she had spent the last half decade cultivating. "I have taken in two cubs, and they will remain under my protection. No challenge is implied. Do you have Alysia or don't you?"

The question spilled out without her thinking about it.

This wasn't the time or place to ask, not with Kral in this kind of mood, but it was Sarik's fault that Alysia had been caught up in this in the first place.

"Both of you seem very concerned about the human," Kral remarked, before again shifting back to the topic he cared about. "You don't think I should consider your actions a challenge to my authority?"

A day before, she had had an answer to that, hadn't she? Now she couldn't seem to find any words. Standing in his presence, she felt like a child again. She fought to keep herself in Sarik's mind, but it was hard while in this place.

"Mistari law says—"

A backhanded blow to the face sent her stumbling back into Christian, and then an open-handed strike made more vicious by claws tore through her shoulder and sent her to her knees.

Her ears ringing and her eyes watering from pain, she looked up at her father.

"You defied my orders when you went after Cori," Kral snarled down at her. "You fled into the night without a word, like a coward, and left others to clean up the mess. You allied with strangers and formed your own tribe with children who I guarantee you will have the strength to overthrow you in the next few years. You are the same arrogant, spoiled child who ran away six years ago, but now you think you can quote Mistari law at me and I will forget everything you've done?"

The words fell on her like hail. She couldn't speak. She couldn't even lift a hand to put pressure on the wound in her shoulder, from which blood was flowing down her arm in a steady stream.

"*Saniet, ohne,*" she whispered. *Mercy, please.*

"Get out," he snapped. "Your room is still as you left it. I will summon you to talk about your 'tribe' when I have time. Christian, stay a minute. We should speak about your misplaced partner."

"You don't have her," Christian said as he offered Sarik a hand up.

The fingers she wrapped around his were numb and streaked with blood. When he helped her up, she could feel how many muscles in her shoulder had been torn open by Kral's claws.

"Judging by the state of Kevin's face and how pissed off you are, I'd say you lost her. That means you have nothing to tell me."

They had barely made it into the hall before Kral said, "Don't make me fetch you, boy." Christian hesitated, turning to meet Kral's gaze. "You may be a witch these days, but that doesn't mean I can't smell the stink of exhaustion on you. You're in no condition to fight me."

Christian went rigid for a moment, then pointedly stepped away from Sarik. "I'll meet you in your room," he said before stepping into Kral's office and closing the door behind him.

White noise. Sarik's head was full of static, like a radio station fading in the distance. There were no words, no thoughts. She leaned against the wall outside Kral's office and was vaguely aware of Kevin as he tended to her shoulder.

Shapeshifters healed fast. Wounds made by another shapeshifter, especially a blood relative, healed a little more slowly, but she still didn't have to worry about permanent scarring or muscle damage. Her father had done worse than this to her.

An outraged voice tried to speak up in her mind, to say *This isn't okay*, but then the voice was muffled.

Her old room. It was cleaner than she'd left it, and someone had fixed the holes she had punched in the black walls, but it still held the attitude of the scared sixteen-year-old brat who had lived there. The antique leather-topped vanity had been stained by a half-dozen colors of nail polish. The elaborately carved handmade ebony headboard had been slashed by an angry adolescent tiger's claws.

The cubs were safe for the moment, and there was nothing more she could do for Alysia unless Christian learned something new from Kral. There were no old friends waiting in the next room for her to say hi to. There was no part of Sahara's life that she wanted to reclaim.

There was only exhaustion and despair. Whatever Christian had done to her earlier had taken its toll, as had the new wounds from her father.

There was nothing to do but wait, so she lay down on the bed. There were no sheets beneath the fuchsia goose-down comforter, but that was fine, because she wasn't in the mood to get that comfortable.

She had barely closed her eyes before she heard the whisper of the door opening and closing, followed by the *snick* of the lock. She didn't need to look to know it was Christian. She could recognize his scent and the fatigued tread of his steps. Besides, who else would bother her here?

"What now?" she asked, staring at the ceiling.

"I don't know," he admitted.

She started to push herself up but stopped when he climbed into the bed next to her, hooked an arm over her waist, and spooned against her back.

"What did he want?" she asked, almost afraid to know.

"As always, he wants too much," Christian answered, "but I can't do anything about that right now. I need rest."

"*Here?*"

"No one is going to bother me here, and *you're* not going to kick me out."

He was right. They wouldn't, couldn't, didn't want to go back to who they had been to each other six years earlier, but at that exact moment, neither of them could be with the person they *did* want to be with.

So she closed her eyes and leaned back against him.

It took her another ten seconds before she thought to ask, "Are you feeding on me?"

"Yes. But I won't hurt you. Go to sleep."

And that's the story of Sahara's life, she thought. *Give with one hand, take with the other.*

As she fell asleep, she realized that for the first time, she understood Jason's refusal to ever feed on her. It didn't matter that it was safe and she was willing. Their relationship hadn't been about use and be used, move ahead and survive at all costs. It had been about more.

I miss you, Jason, she thought.

CHAPTER 19

THE NEXT TIME Alysia woke, she was in a bed, in a non-descript room lit by a basic ceiling light. Next to the bed were six bottles of water, still sealed, and an unopened box of cinnamon-swirl breakfast bars.

Her body still ached, but in a tolerable way, as if she were getting over the flu, not recovering from a puncture wound, an explosion, and a beating.

A moment of panic gripped her, and she dragged her sheets aside to check that both legs were still firmly attached. The leg of her jeans had been cut off above her newly in-jured knee. The ragged edge of denim and the threads hang-ing down had been stained with blood, but the skin itself was intact. She bent the knee experimentally and found that it was stiff but functional, with a shiny new scar just above her kneecap.

She stood cautiously, testing her ability to move. Obviously a witch had been here, but what kind of witch? On whose side?

Her stomach rumbled, and her mouth was bone dry, but no matter how carefully someone had set them out, she wasn't going to help herself to food and water until she knew where she was.

She continued to explore and found a change of clothes on the kitchen counter, a cell phone with a single phone number saved in the contacts list, and, so much more important, all her rank-weapons, with the addition of sheaths for the knives.

The focus on the knives was a good clue about where she was, so she dialed the phone and was rewarded with Ravyn's sleepy drawl. "Yo. You're awake."

"So it seems. Why?"

"You wrecked your stolen car," Ravyn said. "I had to do some quick work to keep you from waking up with a cop by your side. I think I've officially fulfilled my debt to Christian, but the asshole's cell phone was blown up and I don't have another number for him. The witch who worked on you says you should eat and drink when you wake up, or you'll fry your systems and all her work will be wasted."

"Christian's okay?"

"Last I heard. Now I'm going back to bed. There are keys in the fridge."

"Why the fridge?"

"Because I wanted you to call before you split," Ravyn answered. She yawned and then said, "Look, I'm not normally in the business of protecting people, but Kral crossed some lines to get to you, and I owe the leader of Frost a favor for getting him blown up, so you're clear to use the safe house as long as you need it. Also, I don't control members' decisions, but I've strongly suggested to my guild that the number against you is crap. So, I'm done. Have a good day."

She hung up, leaving Alysia shaking her head at the phone. Alysia hadn't known Ravyn well before, but she suspected the burgundy-haired mercenary was going to be an interesting leader.

As assured as she possibly could be that she wasn't going to be poisoned, Alysia double-checked all the packages and seals for any evidence of tampering and then downed two of the energy bars and a bottle of water while she made some phone calls and got the keys from the fridge.

She left messages at the two numbers she knew for Christian, giving him the number of the phone Ravyn had left her and asking him to call. She had half dialed Lynzi before she thought better of it. Until she was sure Kral was off her tail, she didn't want him to have any reason to believe SingleEarth could be used to track her down.

Underneath the keys in the crisper, she found a map marking the location of the safe house and the nearby Crimson guild hall.

The map was good to have because it showed her where

she was, but Crimson wasn't her goal. Her goal was a ranch-style house set well back from the hubbub of the nearest town or major road and surrounded by the forest that seemed to fill so much of New England.

Christian was a city boy at heart, but when it came to his own home, he knew the value of privacy.

His home. Alysia couldn't afford to think of it as hers, even if she had lived there for almost four years. She couldn't automatically assume that she still had any right to it.

Alysia frowned at the sight of the car in the driveway. The shiny silver Prius didn't look like something Christian would drive, unless he had bought it as part of a cover or "borrowed" it in a pinch.

Maybe he sold the house, she thought as she walked up to the front door.

Was some white-picket-fence family playing house in the place where she and Christian had trained together, the place she had come home to after a fight, tired and triumphant?

It was past a normal dinner hour, but not so late that most people would be angry at being disturbed, so Alysia rang the bell. When no one answered, she walked around the one-story home, trying to keep out of sight of the large-paned windows facing the backyard just in case someone was inside. At the sliding glass door to the backyard she paused again, this time to listen. *Anyone there?*

She thought she heard movement, so before breaking in, she tried knocking again.

A kid came to the door. He didn't open it, but he pushed the curtains aside to peer out.

He did *sell it*, she thought, before the kid met her gaze with his own direct stare and she realized who he was. She hadn't seen him long, but she was sure this was the kid who had saved her life at SingleEarth.

A second boy trotted up, wide-eyed and curious, but the older tiger turned, snapped something to him, and then dropped the curtain and walked away.

Don't jump to conclusions, she tried to tell herself as she limped back to her car. She was breathing heavily by the time she reached it, and her knee was aching. She hadn't intended to do this much running around. *But, Christian, why are your ex-girlfriend's adopted kids in your house?*

It didn't take long to pop the lock on the Prius and find Sarik's registration in the glove box. They had dropped her car off and taken one of his, probably to avoid bringing her nice, legal, shiny lease to Onyx, which was almost certainly where they were.

I was right.

Maybe she would head to Crimson after all. Frost was Christian's guild, but it was also the guild whose members were most likely to accept a capture. Very few Crimson members had any interest in kidnappings—in fact, the offer of such a job usually offended them—and Crimson's guild leader seemed to be no friend of Kral's these days. Alysia could get more information there.

Arriving at the Crimson guild hall, however, felt oddly surreal. It didn't have the same sentiment as Frost, or even Onyx; she had joined mostly because it was challenging, not because she fit their normal profile. She could do some subterfuge when she wanted to, but she didn't like the old-money attitude that Crimson tried to maintain.

The Crimson guild hall was located at the back of a good old-fashioned ranch sitting on seven acres of land, complete with a pair of horses and a bevy of barn cats. There were multiple buildings, but the main training area was inside the larger of two barns—the smaller, of course, was for the horses. The training hall was soundproof and looked nothing like a barn on the inside; instead of a hayloft, it had a ladder that led to the weapons storeroom.

Alysia was halfway up the ladder when someone called her name. It took a moment, but she was able to recall that the woman's name was Yasmin. She had trained and competed to join the guild around the same time Alysia and Christian had.

"Nice to see you're not dead," Yasmin remarked.

"You too," Alysia replied sincerely. "How has it been here? How long has Ravyn been in charge?"

"Adam had a job get rougher than he was ready for," Yasmin said, referring to the man who had been the leader of Crimson when Alysia had left the guild.

Alysia wasn't disappointed to learn he was gone, since with Christian in charge of Frost, that meant two of the three leaders who had hated her and tried to kill her were out of the picture.

"I do not know many details, but I do not believe his mind fully recovered. He did badly at last year's challenge. Two others beat him by miles. Ravyn won after a tiebreaker."

"I'd have thought Christian would have tried to take it by now." It was probably a comment better directed to Christian himself, but Alysia was curious as to what the other guilds were saying. Two years earlier, the guild leaders had feared that Christian and Alysia would take over, enough to put a lot of money into trying to stop them.

"He has Challenged twice here. He won Frost but has not won Crimson. I doubt he will bother to try again, now that Sahara has returned."

"What does that have to do with Christian?"

Yasmin, whose gaze seemed perpetually downcast, looked up. "Gossip is not my area of expertise. I find it useful to discuss who is in charge, not who is sleeping with whom." She must have seen something on Alysia's face, because she added, "You were gone two years, Alysia. None of us know if you will run away again. How much trust do you expect?"

"Sahara was gone much longer," Alysia pointed out.

"If one has the patience to deal with a spoiled child, a positive relationship with Sahara kuloka Kral is considered a good investment."

Was that how Christian saw it?

Was that why he had installed the cubs—and possibly Sahara herself—in his house while Alysia was busy being abducted and tortured?

Survive now. Figure out all the rest later.

"I need to know about the contract for my capture," she said.

"I have that information," Yasmin said. "Kral has not officially canceled the contract yet, but our guild leader has marked it as expired, now that Princess Kitty has returned. I do not know if it is still active in Frost or Onyx."

Most members of Crimson wouldn't have access to information from Frost or Onyx. To use Ben's term, few people in Bruja "multiclassed," learning the skills necessary to succeed in more than one of the guilds. Christian would know, but Christian wasn't answering any of the phone numbers she had for him.

It didn't take Alysia long to find someone who knew the next phone number she could try, one she had never called before but that she suspected might get her in touch with Christian.

Of course, if he did answer the phone, she might need to kill him.

Literally or figuratively, she wasn't sure.

CHAPTER 20

THE SHRILL, PERCUSSIVE ring yanked Sarik from her sleep. Disoriented, at first she just stared at the phone on the nightstand.

Christian put a hand on her shoulder and shoved her down on her face so he could reach over her, answer the phone, and bark, "Hello?" He was met with silence, and after a second hello, he hung up.

"Congratulations," he said, rolling away from Sarik and off the bed. "You've been back six hours and you're already getting crank calls."

"Wonderful," she grumbled. She tried again to sit up, and her head spun. She pressed her palms against her closed eyes, trying to fight the inexplicable pressure that seemed to have pooled in the sockets beneath. The sensation was vaguely reminiscent of the time her father had broken her nose and cheekbone.

"You're fine," Christian said. "If you want, I'll buy you breakfast. Or dinner. Whatever meal this is."

"What?" She slapped his hand away when he offered it, because she realized exactly why she felt like utter crap. "You *jerk*. You said—"

"You're not hurt, just tired. If you had ever had a head cold in your life, you would have felt worse. Just be glad shapeshifters can't get the flu."

Her stomach twisted at the mere mention of food, but she felt miserable enough to ask, "Will food help?"

"Yes."

"Great. You're driving, and buying."

As she stood up, she caught sight of herself in the large vanity mirror. The buttercup-yellow cashmere cardigan that Jason had given her for her birthday had been utterly destroyed by her father's claws. The charcoal-gray wool dress pants were in a similarly stained and rumpled state. She had lost her bone hair-sticks before she had even reached the hospital, and her hair was falling around her face.

"I would like to be able to say I would recognize you anywhere," Christian said as she stared at herself, feeling lost, "but if I had seen you unexpectedly at SingleEarth, I might have walked right by you with nothing more than a vague sense of familiarity."

"That was the point." She started to twist her hair back but then stopped as she realized there wasn't any kind of elastic nearby. Sahara had worn her hair down, wild around her face.

"You changed your coloring. The way you walk. Your accent. You even changed your *perfume*," Christian remarked.

"And like any good Onyx boy, you use all your senses," she replied.

To hell with it, she decided. *Play the part, just until you can figure out how to disappear without someone else taking the fall for it.*

She went to the closet and was met by the scent of leather polish. Like most Mistari, she wore primarily materials produced by animals. As Sarik, that meant materials like silk, cashmere, and wool. As Sahara, it had mostly meant patent leather, which addressed the angry-sixteen-year-old-mercenary-brat image and doubled somewhat more practically as armor.

Most Mistari, especially in a group like SingleEarth, had trouble shapeshifting if they wore so much as a polyester scarf or a metal button on their pants. Few could change shape at all with any metal on them, which was why royal-blood Mistari tended to prominently display jewelry as marks of their rank, like the armbands Jeht wore; it meant they were strong enough to tolerate it.

There were steel grommets on Sahara's vest, and the belt she wore low on her hips above her leather jeans was made of twisted white, yellow, and rose gold. In her ears, she wore sixteen white-gold hoops, eight on each side. Christian helped her as she struggled to slip each of them into place with trembling hands. The holes had become smaller since she had left, but they had been made by a firestone needle. They would never completely heal.

She couldn't immediately change the fact that she had highlighted her hair until it was an unextraordinary medium brown, but otherwise the costume was complete once she had slipped on boots with metal stiletto heels she had previously used to kill someone.

"That's a little more familiar," Christian said.

"And you're ever the gentleman for staring while I changed," she replied sarcastically. "What would Alysia think?"

"Contrary to rumors," Christian answered, "Alysia and I are certainly more than 'just friends,' but we were never romantically or physically involved. What would your vampire think?"

She flinched. "What do you know about Jason?"

"Is he the vampire you ran off with while Alysia and I were fighting Maya's entire nest?"

"You were there?"

"I went after you but got there just in time to see you head out the back while I was fighting. The vamp with you was bleeding, limping so badly that it was obvious you were the only thing holding him up. He couldn't have made you go anywhere against your will. Then I found Cori, and I knew why you had gone. I figured if you needed time away, that should be your choice, so I didn't tell Kral I had seen you there. I just told him that I had run into someone from Frost who had already taken down a lot of the nest."

The "someone from Frost" would have been Alysia, of course, but that wasn't the mystery.

"You never told Kral?" she asked.

"It was none of his business."

"How did he find out I was there?" The fact that she had gone after Maya had been one of the crimes he had thrown at her when accusing her of defiance.

Christian shrugged. "I don't know. Information gets around, and gets to Kral, in more ways than we can even imagine."

Very true.

"Such as the fact that Alysia dropped by," Sarik said, "just a few hours before I called."

"That's something I still don't understand," Christian said. "Why did you come to Onyx with her? I'm sure you knew your father wasn't likely to be around at that hour, and you were careful to stay where I couldn't see you, but even with all your camouflage, you risked a lot. You can't tell me you couldn't talk your way out of being there."

"I needed to know if Alysia wanted to kidnap me," she answered vaguely. She could tell that Christian wasn't going to let the subject drop, so she explained, "I knew she was a third-level member of Onyx, not to mention Frost and Crimson. She wasn't dedicated enough to SingleEarth to throw out her weapons, and Crimson especially is known for doing long undercover jobs. If she was there for me, going with her to Onyx seemed the best way to get her to show her stripes where no one else from SingleEarth would get hurt."

"Also the best way to get you noticed and hauled back home."

She laughed. "Sure," she said sarcastically. "I don't care how good Alysia is. I'm three hundred pounds in my tiger form, with the claws and teeth to match. If she had made a grab for me or pulled a weapon, I would have been gone before she made another move. She even let me drive. If it hadn't been for your obsession with her, everyone at Onyx would have told SingleEarth to screw themselves, and I would have known Alysia wasn't after me."

"Obsession?" Christian echoed, looking amused.

She sighed. "I need to ask you for something."

"That lunch I promised?" he quipped.

She shook her head. This was almost as hard as standing up to her father, but if six years in SingleEarth had taught her anything, it was that it was always easier to find the courage to help someone *else* than it was to help herself.

"I want you to leave Alysia alone," she said.

"You really think you can enforce your father's threats? I know you too well, darling."

The words confused her. "What are you talking about?"

"Are you going to try to convince me that you don't know your father agreed to leave Alysia alone and drop the contract against her *only* if she and I didn't get back together?"

"Why would— It doesn't matter," she said. She didn't understand why her father would be so afraid of Alysia, but at that moment, it worked in her favor. "I don't care about my father's issues with Alysia. I care about *Alysia,* for her own sake. She has dreams, Christian. Plans for her life. She can have a future in SingleEarth, or anywhere she wants. If you go find her now, you'll push her to give all that up before she has a chance to realize that she has options. Did you know she's in college?"

Christian frowned, not disapproving but obviously confused. Of course, he and Sahara had been homeschooled by the same tutors; they were literate and could pass for educated, but neither had gone through the traditional school system.

"Tell me you'll give her time," Sarik said.

He looked like he wanted to argue, but at last just shook his head. "I'll tell you the same thing I told your father: I don't control Alysia. Once I confirm with Ravyn that she's all right, I'll back off—for now—but that won't stop Alysia from hunting you down once she recovers and finds out that you and Kral have decided to team up and emotionally blackmail me."

"That's a risk I'm willing to take."

Given what Sarik had put her through, Alysia deserved to take any shot she wanted.

"Also, you've lost your free lunch," Christian added before storming out.

She hesitated for a moment, then followed him, not in the hope of catching him but because the only alternative was continuing to hide in her room.

Near her father's office, however, she saw a sight that enraged her: Kevin, her father's current favorite flunky, leading Jeht and Quean across the dimly lit chamber. Jeht walked ahead of the messenger, perfectly composed, as if completely unaware or uncaring of the grandeur of the Onyx Hall. His brother looked distinctly more nervous, as if he were less trusting of the stranger.

Christian had reached the scene first and was staring at Kevin with murderous intent. "You went to my house?" Christian demanded.

Jeht, meanwhile, caught sight of Sarik. His eyes widened as he took in the change in her appearance—especially the addition of what was probably more metal than he had ever seen another tiger wear.

"What are they doing here?" Sarik asked Kevin, her voice every bit as sharp as Christian's.

Kevin flinched, explaining quickly, "Kral sent me for them. He gave me a message to repeat, in their language. They came with me."

"*Divai, ona,*" Jeht said, his voice questioning but his words formal.

"*Gen'maen'gah'la,*" Sarik replied. Literally, it meant "You are within my sight," spoken as a leader to a lesser tiger in the clan. To Kevin, she added, "My father has no right to bring them here."

"You can tell him that," Kevin replied. "I'm just—"

He broke off as the door to Kral's office opened and the leader of Onyx emerged.

"*Mik'ra,*" Sahara greeted him, not by title but simply as *Father.* "Why have you summoned my—"

"*Your . . . what?*" he replied, using the informal pronoun instead of the formal one she had used for him. The exchange was short, but she could see Jeht contemplate it and guess what it meant: she had backed down and failed to declare herself independent from her father.

And this wasn't a time or place where she could reengage that fight. Christian was watching her, waiting for her to speak up, but she knew that challenging her father at that moment, in his own territory, would only get the boys killed.

Jeht prodded his brother, and Quean knelt before Kral in a Mistari's submissive pose, both knees on the floor, head bowed, and wrists crossed with palms up. Symbolically, the posture said that they were ready to receive with open hands anything their leader was willing to give—even if that was a knife across the bared wrists.

Jeht, on the other hand, met Kral's gaze squarely, then bowed his head and offered his hands as his brother had without sinking to the same level. The choice was intentional, and telling. He was aware that he was not in charge here, but he may as well have said aloud *I'm not certain that you are, either.*

Kral and Jeht regarded each other stoically, the three-hundred-year-old guild leader and the nine-year-old princeling. Somewhere down the line, if Kral couldn't tame him, Jeht *would* be a threat. Sarik tensed, wondering whether her father would feel forced to strike Jeht down and whether she would be able to do anything if he tried.

Aware that speaking out of place and saying the wrong thing might earn her a beating, Sahara chose her words with care. "If he's too much of a risk, no one will fault you for refusing him. His other king did."

Kral responded exactly as she had hoped he would, with pride and showmanship. He turned his back and said as he returned to his office, "They may stay. Sahara, show them around."

The instant Kral was gone, Jeht crossed his arms, and Sarik realized he was trembling. He knew how to play the game, but that didn't mean it didn't frighten him. He had fully expected Kral to kill him for his defiance.

Maybe he would have been glad it was over.

What Jeht didn't know was that, unlike in a Mistari tribe,

the challenge he posed wouldn't necessarily be dealt with directly. A child in Onyx lived a dangerous life. Sahara and Christian knew that.

Cori had known that, too, Sarik thought as Jeht pulled his brother close and leaned his chin on the four-year-old's head, hiding his fear from Quean but unable to hide it from the rest of the world.

CHAPTER 21

MAYBE IT WAS childish, but the moment Christian had answered Sahara's private phone, Alysia had lost all desire to speak to him. She would wait until they were standing face to face, so she could see his expression and try to understand *anything* going through his crazy brain.

From the moment they had met, they had *clicked*. Despite completely different backgrounds and goals, they had always worked well together. Together they had decided to do what no one else had done: join all three guilds and say "screw you" to the rules. It was all about the challenge—it was *always* about the challenge.

It had been for Alysia, anyway, until the day she had joined SingleEarth, and for the first time, the challenge had been paired with something else: expectations. Responsibility, not just for one moment and one contract, but for *people,* day after day, who knew her name and smiled at her in the hallway and relied on her to do her job. Her first two-weeks' paycheck was worth less than she would have charged for two hours' work in Bruja, but something about that stupid check, and the way it said her last name on the top—her *real* last name, the one she'd gotten from her father, which not even Christian knew—convinced her to stay not just two weeks, but two *years.*

Fish gotta swim, birds gotta fly, but what about someone who is a little bit of both? Where did she want to go now? Back to the Crimson safe house, which was apparently the only place she could stay unless she wanted to crash like a fifth wheel with Christian and Sahara and the kids? Back to SingleEarth, so she could explain why they had been shot at and where Sarik had gone?

A temporary solution was suggested to her as her phone chirped, alerting her to a text message: *The contract against you was just dropped at Frost.*

That was vaguely unsettling, as the only person who should have had that cell number was Ravyn, but Ravyn wouldn't have known anything about what contracts were or were not up in Frost. Alysia would have suspected that the information came from Christian if she hadn't had recent evidence that he had been sleeping at Onyx just before the message arrived.

Trap? she wondered.

Possibly, but she had to risk it.

Besides, Frost called to her. It had been hers before she had met Christian.

Each of the Bruja halls had its own style. Onyx had its con-
verted theater, Crimson had its farm, and the Bruja guild hall,
which was mostly only used for events like the competition for
guild leadership, was a redbrick house with white shutters.
The Frost guild hall was in the middle of a quaint suburban
neighborhood; it consisted of four middle-class homes connected by underground tunnels. Frost had been known to call
the local police on guild members who were stupid enough to
look out of place as they approached.

The key to the front door was still hidden in a planter, but
the elaborate computer setup that had occupied the "office"
on the first floor had been replaced by a home theater that
would surely have been the envy of the neighborhood even if
the screen hadn't been an interactive whiteboard—a touch-
sensitive computer screen, like a giant tablet. When Alysia
touched the screen, it flickered to life and showed all of Frost's
current job listings.

Nice upgrade, she thought as she quickly confirmed that the
contract against her was gone. Nearby, she spotted a digital
pen. On the off chance that the operator was currently logged
on, she wrote on the screen, *Did current leader install the new
tech?* If Christian had done this, she would have to reassess his
competency as Frost's leader.

She waited, wondering if the board operator would reply.

The individual responsible for controlling the board was
an utter enigma. No one knew who he or she was. The system
itself probably wasn't *actually* hacker-proof—nothing really
was—but no one ever discouraged members from blatantly
trying to mess with it, and yet to Alysia's knowledge no one

had ever broken in. She was one of many who had tried with no success.

Alysia had almost decided the operator wasn't attending the board when a picture spun into place: a kitten, tangled in computer wires, with a caption saying *WHICH ONE CONTROLS THE INTERTUBES?* Beneath it, words began to appear as they were swiftly typed elsewhere.

fearless leader bolted the door for three hrs so he could figure how to use the new system.

Alysia snickered. That was sad. Predictable, but sad.

you looking for a job? the operator asked.

Yeah. Something nØØb-level.

She needed to start small, because she was out of shape and out of practice, and it would take her a while to catch up enough electronically that she could take on one of the more exciting jobs in that realm. Two years was a very long time in the computer world; she had kept up with reading and research while at SingleEarth, but that wasn't the same as knowing all the ins and outs and back doors of modern technology. She would also have to make new contacts for obtaining documents, since she didn't have access to SingleEarth's specialists, who for altruistic reasons made identification papers, passports, and the like for needy individuals.

this one looks relevant to your interests.

A new listing rose to the top.

Retrieval: Heirloom painting and frame with ritual and sentimental value. Reward offered higher than assessed value of materials. 5,000, method of payment negotiable.

"Ritual value" implied that the work was in some way imbued with magic. Including information about the assessment value was the client's way of ensuring that the mercenary who picked the painting up didn't try to sell it for parts, which for magic items could include anything from enchanted charcoal bits to diamonds and platinum. The reward was ridiculously low for a ritual item, which meant Alysia would definitely have a third party assess it before she turned it in, but its value could be more on the sentimental side. A low reward like that normally suggested an easy job, too, which she hoped would be within her current abilities.

Intrigued, she kept reading.

Last seen in possession of Maya. Previous owner Kral kuloka Kral. Painting lost in a bet six years ago.

That could explain why the board's operator had thought Alysia would be interested. Accepting the job might be suicidal, though, unless the painting was somewhere Maya wasn't guarding.

Alysia reached to tap the *Client* button but found little in the way of useful information.

Client: Anonymous, paid escrow. That meant he or she probably wasn't well known by the guild but had already put five thousand cash into an account as a deposit.

Mostly for curiosity's sake, she tapped the button for more information, including a description of the piece:

10 x 10 inches, abstract painting, with detail in silver and gold thread. Frame is dark wood with silver details and black and red stones. Difficult for most individuals to look at directly.

Well, *that* was interesting.

Has guild leader seen this? she wrote, using the digital pen.

It was doubtful that Christian had bothered to read such a low-level post, but if he had, he might have noticed the same thing Alysia had: this painting wasn't with Maya. In fact, Alysia had seen it, recently, in Kral's little torture chamber.

has not returned to frost hall since posting, the operator replied.

Alysia was a third-level member of Onyx; she had every right to enter the Hall itself, and unless Kral currently had someone in there, the interrogation room was probably unguarded.

One phrase from the posting particularly intrigued her, that bit about how the painting had been "lost in a bet six years ago."

Apparently, a lot of important things had happened six years earlier.

With a shrug, Alysia wrote, *Looking into it.* It wasn't a guarantee she would take the job, but it would let the client know that someone was considering the possibility. For the moderator, she added, *Thanks.*

you were good before you disappeared don't disappoint now, the operator replied, before erasing both that reply and Alysia's thank-you.

There were a few questions Alysia needed answered before she went after the prize.

For one, she wanted to know why Kral had been making bets with Maya in the first place. He didn't seem like the gambling type, and if he was going to start, it probably wouldn't be with a mercenary of Maya's caliber, or with stakes as low as a 5K ritual-item painting that neither he nor Maya was likely to have any use for.

A second issue with the scenario was that Maya had been hired to kidnap Kral's youngest daughter, Cori, right around the time the painting had supposedly entered Maya's possession. It was reasonable that she might have returned it to him along with other items of value as part of an attempt to gain forgiveness and curry his favor after Cori's death, but to someone like Kral, five thousand dollars was more of an insult than a gift.

There is one more thing, Alysia thought as she started to turn away from the board and then turned back. Once again using the pen, she wrote, *Ben?*

Was it possible? Ben had seemed about twenty years old, at *most*. Granted, Alysia had joined Frost when she was fourteen, but Sarta had assigned the Frost operator eight years ago, and as far as Alysia could tell, the individual running the boards hadn't changed since. Ben wouldn't even have been in his teens yet.

She didn't completely discount the possibility. There were plenty of reasons why a member of Bruja might look younger than he was, and the operator's lack of respect for Christian made it easy to believe he had never bothered to introduce himself to the guild's new leader.

Alysia waited by the board until it turned itself off due to lack of activity. Either the operator had wandered off, or he just wasn't inclined to confirm or deny his identity.

It was a mystery that had to wait for another day. She had other work to do, starting with a phone call she really didn't want to make.

She stepped into one of the upstairs bedrooms and closed

the door behind her before she took out her cell phone and dialed a number she had recently memorized. Like most of the rooms in the house, this one was soundproof, so she had no fear that other members might overhear her.

A wary voice answered. "Hello?"

"Jason? This is Alysia. I—"

He interrupted her with a rush of questions. "Alysia! Are you okay? Is Sarik—Sahara—okay? Do you need anything?"

Relief and guilt washed over her, freeing an inappropriate giggle from her throat. "I'm more or less okay, and as far as I know, Sahara is, too," she answered. "She's back at Onyx." *With Christian.* Jason didn't need to know that part. "I had no idea who she was, but her father apparently decided I did. He's the one who put out the contract to kidnap me, to try to find her. Now that we're both gone, he shouldn't have any more reason to harass SingleEarth."

Jason let out a slow breath, an odd self-calming habit for a vampire. "I know we all kept saying we didn't want to force a direct confrontation between SingleEarth and Bruja. None of us realized we were saying we wouldn't protect you. If you want to come back—"

"I don't know what I want right now," Alysia interrupted. "And I don't know what Sahara wants," she added, since she suspected that was really what Jason wanted to know. "I actually have a question for you. An awkward one, but it's eating at me."

"Go ahead."

"You used to work for Maya, right?"

Silence. Alysia remembered what Jason had said when

she had first asked if anyone at Haven #4 knew of Onyx. She remembered his tone when he referred to the woman he "worked for."

Eventually, he replied, "Yes."

"Do you know anything about a painting she received? Small, magical, metal and stone accents. If I'm right about my time lines, it would have been around the time you and Saha— Sarik hooked up, but I'm not sure if it was before or after."

They both kept tripping over that name. Who *was* the tiger these days? If she had gone back to Onyx just to protect SingleEarth, then did she need rescuing? Or did she have her own plan? Was Christian in on it? What the hell was going on?

"I remember it," Jason replied, his voice sounding very quiet and far away. "The magic has something to do with how the body feels pain, how it processes it and responds to it." That explained why Kral kept the thing in his torture chamber. Jason added, "Maya received it as payment for the last job I was ever involved in."

"What was the job?"

And if it went to Maya, why does Kral have it now?

CHAPTER 22

CHRISTIAN GRABBED KEVIN'S arm before the human could sneak away, and hissed, "If you *ever* go to my home again, I will end you. Do you believe me?"

Kevin nodded, but protested, "But Kral—"

"I don't care who your boss is," Christian snarled. "You crossed a line. Cross it again and I can do worse to you than Kral ever could."

Sarik listened to the threats and felt a pit open in her stomach. She was back in a world where one's threat meant everything. If Kevin believed Christian, then the balance of power would shift a little. If he didn't, if he thought Christian's threat didn't have teeth, then he would see the words as an idle bluff.

"Do you know," she said to Christian, though he was too busy watching Kevin slink off into the darkness to care, "I sat at the mediator's table at SingleEarth Haven Number Four for almost a year. I counseled a survivor of foster-care child abuse who killed her parents the first time she shapeshifted." She shuddered, recalling that poor child's guilt, anger, terror, and grief. "I worked with a twenty-year-old human-born Pakana who had been institutionalized since he was eleven, who had blinded himself in his madness four years before, and when he changed shape for the first time, it healed his sight. I have talked people down from bridges and back from windows, found appropriate guardians for orphaned shapeshifter children, negotiated with lawyers and police and the royal houses of every remaining shapeshifter kingdom except the Mistari Disa herself."

She hadn't thought Christian was listening, until he said, "And then you shot your boyfriend and ran away."

"I didn't . . ."

Christian shrugged. "I'm Bruja, darling. I'm the last person to criticize you for looking out for yourself first and screw the rest of the world. Just tell me: if you were so happy being *that* person, then what the hell are you doing here?" He looked at the two cubs, who were watching the discussion with deferential curiosity, probably trying to make sense of the power dynamics. "And why did you bring *them*?"

"You know what my father would do if I went back and SingleEarth tried to protect me," she replied.

"Personally, I wouldn't want to cross SingleEarth," Christian replied. "They don't have a lot of force on their side, but their political power either already does or will soon rival Bruja's."

"That's impossible."

Christian shook his head. "The old leaders, including Kral, pushed hard to keep Bruja 'true to its roots.' Which means they passed up a lot of opportunities."

"Alysia?" Jeht said, his voice breaking into their conversation.

"What?"

"Don't mind me." The human's voice came from the shadows nearby. Sarik hadn't been paying attention to anyone around them, and neither, apparently, had Christian, but Jeht must have scented her and recalled her from SingleEarth.

"Alysia, what are you *doing* here?" Sarik asked, now stretching her awareness to her surroundings. She didn't think anyone else was near enough to overhear if they kept their voices down.

"Eavesdropping," Alysia answered. "I should have guessed you shot Jason, Ben, and Israel." Alysia's voice dripped with all the disdain Sarik had expected.

She protested, "You don't understand."

"*What* don't I understand?" Alysia replied. "You shot your *boyfriend* in what I assume was an attempt to frame me. What the hell was going through your furry brain?"

"Alysia," Christian said, stepping between the two women, "now might not be the best time to—"

"No," Sarik interrupted, "now's good."

"Are you in danger?" Jeht asked, his voice pitched just for Sarik.

"I hope not," she replied, in his language, before speaking quickly to Alysia. "I knew you were from Bruja, all right?" she hissed. "Your file looked suspicious enough that when you moved in, I searched your belongings. What would you have thought if you were at SingleEarth and you suddenly found third-rank weapons from Crimson, Onyx, *and* Frost? I've never even heard of anyone that highly ranked in more than one guild, much less three."

"I would have assumed someone like that was at Single-Earth to mess someone up," Alysia answered. "If I had your history, I probably would have jumped to the conclusion that any merc might be there for *me*. I'm just missing how it's a logical next step to shoot your boyfriend."

"I *panicked*, okay?" Sarik snapped. "I had you in my sights, but then I couldn't go through with the kill. I thought I could frame you, or scare you off, or all sorts of stupid things. I shot at people I could barely see because it was easier than killing someone I could put a name and a face to. I thought you would run once you realized you were being targeted, or that if you turned to fight, someone like Lynzi would take you down. The last thing I expected was for you to jump forward to protect people." Softly, she added, "I didn't *know* you. How could I? You're not like any member of Bruja I ever knew."

"Fair point," Christian observed, breaking into the conversation.

"You understand you acted like a complete idiot?" Alysia asked Sarik.

Sarik nodded. "I hear you bring that out in people."

Christian snickered, and Sarik glared at him before asking Alysia, "Why is my father so afraid of you?"

Alysia shrugged. "He's afraid of a lot of things."

Kral had terrorized almost everyone around him for centuries, but for some reason, Alysia had him scared. "He offered two million dollars two years ago to get rid of you," Sarik pointed out.

"Very flattering," Alysia replied, "but I didn't do anything you don't know about. Kral's a few hundred years old, and he has some gray hairs hiding under the Clairol for Men. The world moves on, but he won't. He's afraid of the modern world. He's afraid of technology. And more than anything, he's afraid of getting old and seeing someone younger—especially someone human—take what he built and change it from his image. He focused on me because I showed up when you disappeared. I'm the peppy human girl who replaced his carefully groomed, perfect heir. But the reality is, if it's not me, it's just going to be someone else." She looked around to where movement in the shadows made it clear that some of the novices were getting brave enough to creep closer, trying to overhear their conversation. "Can I talk to you two somewhere a bit more private?"

"Sure," Christian said.

"We can talk in my room," Sarik said, feeling much the way she had when Alysia had first interviewed at SingleEarth: as if the following conversation might change her entire world.

Hopefully I can handle things better this time, she thought, before saying to Jeht, "I know you don't understand what's going on. Don't jump to any conclusions."

"I'm not objecting," Christian said, "but just so everyone is aware, Kral may go insane if he hears that the three of us ducked into Sahara's room together and one of us didn't come out a corpse."

"If you take Quean with you, I'll guard the door," Jeht said, guessing correctly that they wanted their conversation private.

"Don't fight anyone who comes up," Sarik told him. "Just knock."

Jeht nodded. She had never intended to let him *actually* fill his role as her guard, but here she was, with a nine-year-old standing watch while she led the others inside and shut and locked the door. Quean sat in the corner, watching but instinctively staying out of the way. Alysia dropped the bag she had been carrying onto the bed and opened the top to reveal a small, familiar work of art.

The piece was ten inches square, painted, with an addition of silver leaf and finely embroidered threads Sarik happened to know were pure gold firestone. The frame was a combination of ebony wood and platinum designs she couldn't make sense of because her eyes hurt when she looked at them. The gemstones set into the piece were not firestone, but rather a red diamond, a scarlet emerald, and then lines of black opal.

She was familiar with the work, of course, because it belonged to her father. It normally hung in his office or his interrogation room.

"How did you get that?" she asked.

"Broke into the greenroom and picked it up," Alysia

answered blithely. "His entire security system consists of a guy named Kevin."

"The rest of his security system relies on the fact that most people in Onyx are not stupid enough to steal from him," Christian pointed out. "I'm assuming you have good reason to flash it in front of his daughter."

"Tell me, what's this thing valued at?"

"The gems alone could be sold for over a million," Christian answered promptly, "but you can't peel them off without breaking the spell first, and it was beyond my abilities the last time I tried." At Sarik's shocked look, he added, "I'm not dumb enough to try to sell the whole piece. It's too recognizable. The stones alone could be sold to any human jeweler who wasn't too particular about asking their history."

"Seven years ago, I bought a piece of gold firestone thread just about half a yard long from Pandora for fifteen thousand dollars," Sarik volunteered, resigned. "That was with her 'Onyx discount.' It's unbreakable, fine enough and light enough to fold anywhere, can be woven into a piece of rope to make bonds even a vampire can't escape, and can be made into a garrote that will kill almost anything instantly. And Pandora is the only Triste I know who makes it, so it's something of a seller's market."

"Any thoughts?" Alysia asked, handing it to Christian.

"Sure," he answered. He took the painting but then set it in his lap instead of looking at it. "My thought is, you have a good reason to ask. So share."

"There's a contract up in Frost," Alysia explained, "offering five K for this thing. When I read the offer, I vaguely recalled the painting, but I didn't remember it well enough to know what it was made of, and the description just said things like 'metal and wood frame' and 'red and black stones.' But it matches perfectly."

"Five thousand wouldn't cover the risk of walking in to pick it up," Christian answered. "I've heard of clients trying to swindle mercs by offering a lower price than an item is worth, but any idiot can tell this is worth more than that."

"Who was the client?" Sahara asked. "Maybe he just wanted to bring my father down a notch by having it stolen and doesn't actually care if you turn around and sell it."

"Maybe," Alysia said, "but then there's the question of where it's been. The item history on the number said Kral lost it in a bet with Maya, but I spoke to—" She hesitated. "I confirmed that it was in fact in Maya's possession briefly, six years ago."

"Kral lost a multimillion-dollar ritual item in a bet with a mercenary?" Christian scoffed. "Not likely. That painting has been around since we were . . . what, five or six?" he asked, turning to Sarik. She nodded. "And I would have noticed if it hadn't been back in his office the next time I saw him after that job, which was . . . oh, two days later, something like that."

"Why would you give a valuable, highly recognizable item to a mercenary?" Alysia asked. "Someone please tell me I'm wrong about what I'm thinking."

"You'd use something like this if you wanted to pay for an important job but the merc was worried about getting nailed for it later," Christian said. His voice had become heavy, and he was looking at Sarik with something akin to horror. "You'd

use something people would recognize as yours so the mercenary could later say 'I did this with your blessing' if you tried
to blame them."

"And if that mercenary screwed up royally?" Alysia
prompted.

"They would return the item."

Sarik was listening, but she wasn't listening, because what
Alysia was suggesting was . . .

"My father didn't kill Cori."

But how many times had Kral told her that Cori was her
weakness?

Cori, poor human Cori. Cori, who was the only living
proof that Kral *himself* had human blood, because a pureblood
shapeshifter couldn't have a human child even with a human
mother.

She looked at Quean, who was sitting on the floor and
staring up at her with awe and trust. He didn't understand a
word they were saying. Didn't understand that his new king
had hired mercenaries to torture an eleven-year-old girl to
death in an attempt to bring his other daughter back in line.
Had Kral planned to "rescue" Cori at the last minute, to prove
he was stronger than Sahara, but then Maya's boys had gotten
carried away? Or had he just planned to let Sahara find Cori's
mangled body so she would know how completely she had
failed?

Knowing he had hired Maya even explained why Kral had
assumed that Alysia was responsible for Sahara's disappear-
ance. He knew Sahara had been there, because Maya had told
him. He also knew that because Maya was on his payroll, she

wouldn't have hurt Sahara. Alysia was the only other person he could blame. And he did.

"Christian," Sarik said softly, "I know you are not here entirely of your own will, and it may not be entirely in your own interest, but . . ." The expression he gave her at that preamble almost made her stop, but she gulped and finished. "Will you stand beside me *a'maenke*?"

Christian frowned, probably trying to remember what the term meant, and then he looked at Alysia. He nodded and answered, "Once. Then I'm gone."

"What's the plan?" Alysia asked.

"Christian can explain," Sahara answered. "I'm going to tell Jeht, and then . . . and then I need to find my father."

CHAPTER 23

CHRISTIAN *COULD* EXPLAIN, but now that he had Alysia alone, he had another, more pressing question he wanted answered first.

"What's your plan, Alysia?"

She looked at him like he was crazy, which he certainly deserved, and said, "I'm not the one with a plan right now."

She has dreams. Did you know she's in college?

"You left SingleEarth because of the attacks," Christian said. "The attacks were the result of Sahara being there. She isn't there anymore."

It was the most direct way he could express the thoughts going through his head, because every fiber of his being was shouting, *You idiot! If Alysia wanted to live in SingleEarth, she would be there. It isn't like she needs your permission.*

"Are you saying I should go back?" Alysia asked.

"I'm saying..." What *was* he saying? "It's not a life I would choose for myself, but if it's what *you* want... What I'm asking is, do you *want* to stay in Bruja?"

She hesitated, her gaze going distant. "Yes," she answered, even though her tone said, *I don't know.* Instead of explaining, she asked, "Do you know who runs the Frost board?"

The question was so out of left field that Christian thought at first he had misheard. "The Frost board?"

"The operator," Alysia clarified. "The person who actually writes the posts. It's not you."

He shook his head. "I don't have a clue. But I know he doesn't like me."

For weeks after Christian had won leadership in Frost, posts had randomly appeared on the board accusing him of killing Alysia so she wouldn't compete against him.

Alysia smiled, but it was a distant expression. "You know that if I stay, once I'm back in shape, I'll challenge you for Frost."

"Why?" He tried to keep his voice utterly neutral as he asked what seemed like one of the most important questions he had ever uttered. Did Alysia really want the guild, or did she just want to get back at him?

"Because..." Was it just for the challenge? Because she was pissed at him for staying with Sahara, something he hadn't yet had a chance to explain? Because she didn't know what else to do? Any of those reasons would tell him she didn't really want to be there. She looked up and met his gaze squarely as she said, "Because you're wrong for Frost. You're flashy and she's subtle. You're arrogant and she's whatever she needs to be at any moment. You're a bear; she's a bear trap hidden in the woods."

"And apparently 'she' is a girl," Christian quipped, relaxing.

"You joke, but you know I'm right," Alysia asserted. "I don't know if Frost will have me back, but damn it, I know we need someone who doesn't take three hours to figure out a giant tablet."

There it was again—"*we*." And this time it meant Frost.

"Let's see what happens at Onyx, and then we'll see about getting you in shape for Frost," he replied.

"Are you going to tell me what's going on? I gather Sarik is going after Kral."

"Normally," Christian admitted, "when Sahara stands up to Kral, she backs down fast. This time? I don't know." He had seen the expression on her face. He knew better than anyone what Cori had meant to her. Beyond that, he knew she had noticed the way Kral had looked at Jeht. He explained, "She asked me to stand with her, which means she intends to challenge him within Mistari law, which she has on her side."

Bruja rules were a little hazy, but generally, attacking guild leaders was frowned upon and not a way to earn guild leadership. On the other hand, Onyx wasn't like the other guilds. Few people competed at Challenge. If Kral fell under

Mistari law, Christian suspected that Sarta and Ravyn—the rest of the leadership—would accept it, if only because it was the result of Kral's own arrogance.

"What does *a'maenke* mean?" Alysia asked as Christian quickly checked his weapons and then, reluctantly, started putting them aside.

"As her mate," he answered with a wry smile. The term was technically applicable even if it was worlds away from describing their current relationship.

Alysia prompted, "Which means what, in this case?"

"A queen's mate is the only one who can share a leadership challenge with her," Christian answered. "Sahara can't take Kral alone and she knows it. Until she declares satisfaction or submission, I'm allowed to fight with her."

"Can you take Kral?" Alysia asked.

That's the twenty-million-dollar question, isn't it?

Christian laid his jacket down on the bed, because it was easier to take it off than to strip all the weapons from it, and because it would count as armor. He would have felt less naked without his pants.

"I really don't know," he answered. "But if Sahara can get the nerve to declare *jeraha* and follow through, then I'm willing to try." His eyes drifted to the painting. "I liked Cori. She was a sweet kid."

He had seen what they'd done to her. Sahara had run away, and he understood why. Christian was the one who had taken Cori's body home to be buried.

"Be my second?" he asked Alysia.

She asked, "What do you need?"

"If Kral uses any weapon beyond his own body, or if any-one else interferes, you can shoot him," he explained.

"Anyone?" Alysia asked. "If this goes down in the middle of Onyx, you're going to have a lot of trigger-happy mercenaries wondering what this means to them."

"Onyx belongs to Kral. If he can't control his people, that's his problem."

"I'm technically one of those people," Alysia pointed out. "Doesn't that mean if I kill him in the middle of the fight, it's his own fault?"

"You're also one of my people through Frost, and arguably one of Sahara's, given the way you two teamed up at Single-Earth," Christian said. "Normally I'm not opposed to splitting hairs or outright cheating, but we don't want to sever Onyx's ties to the Mistari. It's one of the most valuable political connections the guild has. There's no point in taking Onyx if we destroy it in the process."

"*Jeraha* is a fight to the death, isn't it?" Alysia asked.

"Unless the combatants agree otherwise," Christian answered. He couldn't imagine Kral backing down until he was ready for a body bag.

"Just so you know," Alysia said, picking up a couple of his discarded weapons and adding them to her own armament, "I don't give a flying fruitcake about Onyx's ties to the Mistari. If I need to decide between cheating and saving you, or playing fair and letting Kral kill you, you know which way I'll go."

"Yeah," he said, though he also knew that if Kral took him out, it would probably happen too quickly for Alysia to do more than blink.

Kral had been around a long time. Maybe he *was* getting old, but that didn't mean he didn't still know how to fight. Christian could do a lot of damage in mere seconds with a touch, but so could a full-grown tiger.

"Let's go," he said, trying to sound more confident than he felt.

Alysia followed as he left the room. They both paused, blinking, as they entered the dim Onyx Hall.

"Ten to one she chickens out," Christian said softly to Alysia as Kral's voice reached them both through the darkness. He was across the Hall, working with one of the novices. Christian could see Sahara in silhouette as she watched him, the two cubs next to her.

"You might be surprised," Alysia replied.

"Father."

And there was Sahara's voice, holding only the barest tremor. Alysia and Christian both sped their steps to reach the tigers as Kral replied, "Sahara, excellent. I need you to—"

"I need you," Sahara interrupted, raising her voice above his, "to answer a question for me."

Christian wasn't sure, but he thought the continued wavering in the tigress's voice was not just fear, but also fury.

Use that anger, he thought. *Remember what you're fighting for.*

"And I need you to answer honestly," Sahara continued, "because I want to know that you at least have the courage to admit you would sink so low."

Kral turned fully toward his daughter, and the novices who had been nearby backed away fast.

"Child, I suggest you watch your tone."

Sahara ignored the warning and continued with her questions.

"Did you hire Maya to kill Cori?" she asked, not bothering to keep her voice quiet to avoid being overheard. "Did you pay her the equivalent of millions of dollars to torture to death an eleven-year-old human girl? Did you do it to frighten me? Or to teach me a lesson? Did you—" She broke off. "Was she really so threatening, just because she was human?"

There was the accusation Kral could not tolerate: not that he had had his daughter killed, but that her existence had been a *threat* to him.

"You don't know what you're talking about," Kral replied flatly. "Cori was—"

"Cori was my *sister*," Sahara snarled. "She was your *daughter*! She . . . she was your tribe's weakest child, and instead of protecting her, as was your duty, you had her murdered in an underhanded power play because you were worried she made you look weak."

"She was proof that he's mortal," Alysia interjected. "His human blood is kicking in. He's aging. Getting weaker."

Kral's eyes narrowed as he glanced at Alysia. "What is she—"

"Don't look at her!" Sahara nearly shrieked, her voice breaking. "You face me first. Fight anyone else after me if you can, but first you'll answer me: *Did you have Cori killed?*"

"So what if I did?" Kral snapped back. "I thought getting rid of her would make you stronger, but you're still the same impulsive child you've always been."

"I'm not a child anymore."

Kral flat-out laughed. "You are my only daughter, Sahara,"

he said calmly, "so I will give you one last chance to back down. You know you can't win a fight against me, and your so-called mate has never fought a tiger."

Just hit him, Christian thought. *Don't let him talk to you. Don't let him frighten you.*

"I . . ." Sahara hesitated.

"Back down, Daughter," Kral said, "and maybe I will give you a chance to visit the Mistari main camps. You wanted to talk to someone about the boys, didn't you? And it's about time I sent an emissary there to relay my regards."

She wasn't going to do it. She was going to listen to his lies and manipulations. Christian's entire body was tensed, waiting for this fight, and Sahara was weakening before his eyes.

"I've fought a tiger before." The voice from the darkness made Christian jump. "And if I need to, I'll challenge Christian first for the right to stand beside Sarik."

Who the hell are you? he thought, turning toward the vampire who had waltzed into Onyx as if he weren't surrounded by vampire hunters. It had to be Maya's boy. Sahara had called him Jason. Christian had dismissed Jason as the plaything Sahara had picked up to replace him after she left Onyx, but if he was here now, then he had to be a good deal more.

The question was, could he fight?

Sahara's head whipped around to look at the newcomer. She drew a deep breath, as if inhaling strength.

Christian realized that whether or not Jason could fight, what mattered was that he was the inspiration Sahara needed. Christian stepped back, yielding the title of Sahara's "mate" to the man who actually held it.

"I am Sahara kuloka Kral," she said, her voice gaining power, "I am your daughter, and by the blood of the sister who died in my arms, I declare *jeraha*. I stand with my mate beside me. Will you face us?"

"Don't make me hurt you, child."

Icily, Sahara said, "Will you face us, or will you yield?"

In the blink of an eye, the ancient tiger shifted just enough to turn hands to claws and lashed out at Jason. The vampire jumped back with a hiss of pain as his blood splashed across several bystanders.

Alysia took a step forward, but Jeht grabbed her arm. The elder Mistari boy was determined that the laws of his kind be followed.

Meanwhile, Sahara pounced at Kral, her full tiger form causing his human shape to stumble back several steps before he, too, changed, twisting as he fell, until the two tigers separated, both bleeding, with snarls of rage and pain.

"This is insane," Alysia whispered.

"But entertaining," another familiar voice responded.

Sarta. Christian hadn't seen the leader of all three Bruja guilds much since she had taken over the position—unlike Crystalle, Sarta did not believe in micromanagement—but now she seemed to appear out of nowhere, perfectly on time for an unscheduled leadership challenge. "Kevin called me, on Sahara's orders," she explained. "She was right. I do want to see this."

It was worth watching. For SingleEarth mediators sworn to nonviolence, Sahara and Jason fought with a synchronized savagery that could only be described as awesome.

CHAPTER 24

ALYSIA WINCED AS Jason landed a blow on Kral's lower back. With vampiric strength behind it, the double-fisted hit had probably obliterated his kidney. Kral gave a cry of rage and pain and replied with a swipe that took out most of Jason's face, sending him sprawling toward Alysia.

As Alysia instinctively moved toward Jason, she once again felt the viselike grip of the older tiger cub. Jeht looked up at her long enough to shake his head; then he turned his gaze back toward the fight. Sarik pounced, snarled, and darted, keeping Kral's attention on her while Jason wiped blood from his eyes and healed enough to rejoin the fray. The tigers occasionally took their fully feline forms, but most of the time they fought with claws on human hands.

"We're really going to stand here until they manage to beat each other to death?" Alysia whispered to Christian.

Kral was hundreds of years old; he had founded Onyx. Jason had been initiated to violence by Maya, one of the most vicious of the modern mercenaries. And Sahara had been born and raised in this world. They could all dish out pain like SPAM from a can, but they could also heal it.

There had to be *something* Alysia could do. Some way to distract Kral or . . . something! Anything. Kral was nearly double Sahara's size in both human and tiger form. He wasn't going to back down until they killed him.

Screw this. "Look, kid," she said, wondering if the boy would translate her tone even though he couldn't understand her words, "I know this is about kings and queens to you, but to me it's about watching people I kind of like get *pummeled.* That's not the kind of thing I can just let happen."

She wrenched her arm out of the tiger cub's grip. He shouted at her and jumped between her and the fight, pulling a knife from a sheath at his waist and holding it up as if to say *I can't understand your words, and you can't understand mine, but can you understand this?*

"Now, Alysia," Christian said, with all his good-old-boy charm, "you know I'll back your play if you make it, but I *really* do not want to beat up a nine-year-old just to give you a chance to get yourself killed for Sahara freaking kuloka Kral."

"I never knew Sahara," Alysia retorted, "and I—"

Sarik shouted, "Father!" All eyes returned to the fight in time to see Sarik dodge Kral's next swipe of claws and then dance back, choosing not to retaliate. Instead, she demanded breathlessly, "Is this really what you want?"

Jason, ever observant, responded to her change in tactics. He moved back, putting himself out of Kral's easy reach, and stopped pressing the attack.

Kral paused, using the time they were giving him to recover.

Both tigers were winded and flushed, and all three combatants were striped with injuries. During the brief respite, Alysia saw Jason set his teeth and smooth broken ribs and a collarbone back in place; Kral had literally tried to tear his throat out. Kral meanwhile pressed a hand over a wound low on his stomach that was bleeding profusely and threatening to expose organs beneath. Why was Sahara letting him recover? So they could start this all again?

"I missed *Saw 3D* intentionally," Alysia remarked to no one in particular, trying to cover for a twisting stomach.

No one answered, because Sarik started talking.

"You killed Cori," she said, "because she wasn't the child you wanted." Despite her shortness of breath, despite wounds that Alysia could see beginning to knit themselves closed and blood staining the floor around them all, Sarik spoke in an even tone that forced those nearby to hush to listen. "You would kill me now because I am the child you tried to make me and I won't let you rule me. I know that you intend to kill Jeht because you know he will fight you once he is older. Is that all you want with the rest of your life? You are getting older. Someday you will not be strong enough to hold Onyx. Do you really want to leave nothing behind?"

"It is better to leave nothing," Kral retorted, "than to leave a legacy of weakness and—"

"Listen to yourself," Sarik interrupted.

She's going to try to talk him down, Alysia thought incredulously. *She's going to mediate this situation.*

Sarik continued, watching her father warily, never releasing his gaze.

"Onyx is . . . It's a portrait, one that's fading and weakening while you pretend that you will last forever. If you destroy us all now, destroy everyone strong enough to stand against you—me, Jason, Alysia, Christian, Jeht, and even little Quean—you won't be remembered as a powerful tiger who ruled Onyx for centuries. You'll only be remembered by those who are mortal, those whose memories only go far enough to remember when Onyx was weak and run-down and you were seen as the fool who let it get that way and sat on its puppet throne in the last of its years. Or you can move on now and let your legacy stand as a legend. It is your choice."

"I can't do that."

Kral had run Onyx for two hundred years. Did he even know *how* to do anything else?

"Then . . ."

Sarik took a deep breath, and Alysia braced herself, prepared to join the fight. Instead, Sarik knelt and bowed her head, lifting her wrists up before her.

Jason followed her, taking the same posture, followed by the two tiger cubs.

"You can kill us all, or you can let us stand," Sarik said.

He'll never let them go, Alysia thought as Kral growled at his daughter, her mate, and her adopted cubs. *He can't just forget about a challenge like this.*

"Kill us," Sarik continued, "and you end your own blood. You end your line and any chance you have at progeny who will determine the course of this world. Or you can do the bravest thing you have ever done in your life: yield, and allow your children to be strong."

Can I block him before he goes for them? Alysia thought, desperately considering angles, what weapons she had, and how many people would try to get in her way.

She had a knife in her hand when Kral took a step back, then another, and another, each swifter than the last. Only when he was no more than a shadow against the back wall did he say, "Stand, *jeraha'rahvis*. Stand and take your place."

Alysia stared, unbelieving.

Was it over?

"You don't need that," Christian said, touching the back of her hand that held the firestone knife.

"Thanks," Sarik said as Jason helped her to her feet. Then she turned and lifted both of the boys up, the action obviously symbolic. To her father, she said, "You will return to the camps and let the queen know of the changes to the Kral clan?"

"*Sana'kaen*," Kral answered, and turned stiffly to leave, refusing to meet the gaze of any other member of Onyx.

After they all watched Kral slink out the door, Sarta cleared her throat, capturing everyone's attention before she said, "There is still a matter to be addressed here."

Onyx. The confrontation had narrowed down to Sarik,

her father, and her tribe, but there was another world around them wanting to know how it would be changed by these events.

"With permission from the leadership," Sarik said, nodding toward Sarta, "I would recommend an impromptu Challenge in, say, two weeks. I won't compete. Neither will my father. Onyx needs new leadership." She looked at Christian and then turned her gaze to Alysia and asked softly, "What about you?"

Sarta also appeared interested in the answer, which wasn't surprising, since Frost had been her guild for years before Alysia had joined.

"Frost needs new leadership as well. And new direction," Alysia replied, looking up at Sarta, who nodded her approval. Challenge wasn't until next summer; she had time to get into shape before then. To Jason and Sarik, she added, "I'll keep in touch."

Alysia didn't intend to police the morals of her members— most of them would go their own way, as they always had— but SingleEarth was the fastest-growing and most powerful organization in the modern world. It would be madness to let those contacts just drift away.

Besides, Alysia wasn't quite ready to abandon SingleEarth completely. She had learned things there, about life and about herself.

"Then . . . we'll see you around," Jason said warmly, before turning his gaze to Christian to ask, "You and I, we aren't going to have a problem, are we?"

"Only if you try to give her back," Christian replied, earning an exhausted glare from Sarik.

Alysia watched the exchange with amusement. Christian had known Kral's carefully molded daughter, Sahara. Would he ever understand how much she had changed?

"Though, just for the record, you do know she *shot* you, right?" Christian said.

Sarik tensed, but Jason answered, "I figured that out, yes." Yet he didn't take his hand from hers.

"Well, you two crazy kids have fun, then," Christian said.

The group started to break apart, each going their own way. Once Sarik, Jason, Jeht, and Quean were gone, someone asked, "Who's going to clean this up?"

Alysia turned toward Kevin, who was looking despondently at the blood-spattered floor as if it were the worst thing to ever happen to him.

"You asked first, so you get the prize," she replied.

Christian started to ask, "What about—"

He stopped when Alysia's phone buzzed. The text message read, *welcome back, Boss*

A number came up this time, at least, which meant she was able to reply, *Not yet.*

you will be

Ben?

you have a cute obsession with names

It had to be Ben. The Frost operator, always an enigma, could pass as a geeky college frosh.

"Who is it?" Christian asked, impatiently watching her tap buttons on her phone.

"A friend," she replied, "I hope."

I'm planning to turn Frost upside down, she texted. If he wasn't on her side, she was going to be in trouble.

She wanted to make Frost into a modern guild, to go beyond their reputation as brutal assassins. They could partner with SingleEarth, whose document and electronic departments needed the support, and who desperately needed a strong arm from time to time. It wouldn't be a partnership popular with all members, but it would be profitable enough to overcome most reluctance, as long as Alysia had the important people on her side.

i'm with you, Boss, Ben replied.

She shut the phone as Christian approached and wrapped an arm around her waist.

"It's going to be crazy around here for a while," he said. "Kral left Onyx a royal mess. Are you going to stick around to help?"

"I'll be here," she answered. "To help, or hinder, or make all the little Bruja mercs jump like grease on a hot griddle."

"Business as usual, then?"

Chaos and crisis, with a side of piss-people-off and rebuild-the-world.

"Nah," she said, considering, "this will be something completely new."

EPILOGUE

WHAT NEXT? LYNZI wondered. Jason and Sarik had called to say they were on their way back, but Sarik had followed that comment up with a rapid explanation of how she was planning to create a new position for herself and might need to resign as mediator. She hadn't included Jason in the statement, but Lynzi knew that where Sarik went, Jason would follow.

That left Lynzi once again in charge of Haven #4, as she had once been many years ago, when she had granted SingleEarth the right to use her territory as a Haven in the first place.

She stared at the computer screen and started to write the advertisement for an open mediator position six times before

she decided instead to email Joseph, the man who had resigned
at the start of this whole strange fiasco.

> Joseph,
> You resigned from Haven #4 due
> to philosophical objections—you said
> SingleEarth didn't fully understand
> or respect the needs of the nonwitch
> members of our organizations. Recent
> events have given me a new respect for
> your position. Would you be willing
> to meet me, to discuss your ideas? If
> you would be willing to try again, I
> think Haven #4 could be influential in
> changing SingleEarth for the better.
> It's your choice.

⚜

What next? Jeht wondered as he followed his queen back to
the strange campground where he had been living for the last
several days. He smiled to see the one called Mark waiting for
them, looking relieved.

He tried to suppress the smile, which seemed like it might
be weakness, but then couldn't.

His queen spoke to Mark in their language before she sat
heavily on the bench and pulled Quean into her lap. Quean
had fallen asleep in the car and was still sleepy-eyed.

"My tribal name is Kral," she explained in her strangely
musical accent. He understood every word she said in his

language, but the flavor of this place was even in the way she spoke. "We are not a large tribe, but we are respected enough that if you wish, we can visit the main camps, and we can probably find another tribe that would be willing to take you in. It may take a few days to arrange that trip, so you have some time to decide."

He nodded but did not yet speak, because he could tell she had more to say.

"You have another choice," she said. "You can stay here, as part of my tribe. You have seen that the world here is . . . different than in the Mistari camps. It is not as violent, but it can be even more complicated. Staying here would be hard. You would need to learn many things. You will always be Mistari, and now that I am a queen in my own right, you will always have the right to return to the main camps. But you can also be an ambassador. There are not many places where Mistari children can look for help. You learned that the hard way. I plan to change that.

"Think about it," she said. "It's your choice."

❧

What next? "Ben" wondered as he fiddled with Alysia's smartphone. He popped the SIM card out of the back and replaced it with another one he had prepared. A few minutes later, he had uploaded the software she would need to receive instant mobile updates on everything going on in Frost.

"See?" he said. "Easy."

"Sure," she answered. The ironic response was high praise, and he knew it. It meant that she hadn't completely understood his explanation of how the system worked—especially the encryption, which he was particularly proud of. He liked stumping her. "I assume you still want to hang back from the meeting today?"

"Yes and no," he answered.

She gestured for him to continue.

"The SingleEarth IT department asked me to go to the meeting as a technical consult," he explained. "Apparently when I planted my file in their system, I did too good a job. They like Ben a lot."

"What *is* your real name?"

He loved it when she asked that. It made him laugh every time.

This was the first time he'd been able to see her face when she asked, which was neat. She really cared, for some reason. "You'd have to ask my mother that," he replied. "I think you call her Sarta."

Oh yeah, the wide-eyed reaction was absolutely worth it.

"I almost forgot," he said, moving on as if he hadn't left his fearless leader flabbergasted, "we got a request from Onyx to install some Wi-Fi in their guild hall. I know you have a soft spot for the new leader, and I'd love to bug that place—"

"I'll do it myself," Alysia interrupted.

Ben hadn't figured out all her cues yet and wasn't able to tell when she was going to play nice and when she was going to play practical, but he figured there was a fifty-fifty shot that Frost would soon have an awesome audio-and-video feed of all the important spots in the Onyx Hall.

In response to a low beep, he glanced back at the computer

that constantly scrolled through jobs going in and out of Frost. Dealing with the messages had become more complicated since the big showdown at Onyx, as Frost's new leader had wasted no time declaring her vision and pulling guild members after her with the charisma of a black hole.

May you live in interesting times, a fortune cookie had told him once. The little strip of paper was taped to his monitor now. He looked at it and smiled, thinking, *You have no idea, cookie friend. No idea at all.*

"Sure, Boss," he said, typing as he spoke. "It's your choice."

ABOUT THE AUTHOR

AMELIA ATWATER-RHODES WROTE her first novel, *In the Forests of the Night*, when she was thirteen. Other books in the Den of Shadows series are *Demon in My View*, *Shattered Mirror*, *Midnight Predator*, *Persistence of Memory*, *Token of Darkness*, and *All Just Glass*. She has also published the five-volume series The Kiesha'ra: *Hawksong*, a School Library Journal Best Book of the Year and a Voice of Youth Advocates Best Science Fiction, Fantasy, and Horror Selection; *Snakecharm*; *Falcondance*; *Wolfcry*, an IRA-CBC Young Adults' Choice; and *Wyvernhail*. Visit her online at AmeliaAtwaterRhodes.com.

HER BITE IS
YOUR OBSESSION

Amelia Atwater-Rhodes
author of WYVERNHAIL

PERSISTENCE
OF MEMORY

Sixteen-year-old Erin just wants to fit in at her new school, but she's no ordinary teenager. Erin has a secret alter ego, a vampire named Shevaun, who is determined to sever their connection once and for all. . . .

675   AMELIAATWATERRHODES.COM